BOOK 1

BATTLE DRAGONS

CITY OF THIEVES

BOOK 1

BATTLE DRAGONS

CITY OF THIEVES

ALEX LONDON

SCHOLASTIC PRESS

10 9 8 7 6 5 4 3   23 24 25 26

Printed in the U.S.A.   37
This edition first printing 2022
Book design by Maeve Norton

DEDICATED TO ANYONE WHO HAS
TRIED TO TAME A DRAGON, OR
DREAMED THAT THEY MIGHT.

PART ONE

"WHAT WOULD DR. DRAGO DO?"

PART ONE

1

AT MIDNIGHT THEY'D LIGHT THE sky on fire. Abel stayed up to watch, keeping himself awake by reorganizing DrakoTek cards on his bed.

Frostspitter with alloy armor: +2 against Firemouths
Wyvern with tail flamethrower: +2 attack, -1 speed

Ugh.

He already had three of those wyverns, and they were too slow to do any good in a game. They were fast in close combat but slow in straightaways. Their poison breath couldn't hurt other dragons, only the riders, and the flamethrower at the tail wasn't all that useful. Anyone with a booster card or just a faster dragon from a premium deck could outrun and outfight a wyvern like that. Abel had no premium decks.

He rearranged the grid of cards on the bed so that the Frostspitter got the flamethrower and the wyvern got the alloy armor. In a real dragon battle, a wyvern could have both, but the game only let you mod your dragon once, unless you had bonus storage cards. Abel did not. Those came with the premium decks too, and his parents couldn't afford to buy them. He could've won some off another player, but he only ever played with Roa, and he never won against his best friend. They were a way better player than he was.

He wished he hadn't lost his Green Frost dragon with

diamond blades to Roa last week. He'd have to plan for a rematch, though he doubted he'd win that either. Sometimes, while they were playing, Roa would try to keep him from losing by offering advice or reminding him about a dragon's special skills, but he was reckless. Play first and ask questions later, that was Abel's philosophy.

"And that's why I always lose," he told himself, yawning. It was 11:57. He could do this. He could stay awake.

Percy snored in a ball at his feet. The pangolin's warm scales rested on his ankles. Somehow, his cuddly, scaled pet could curl into a ball and take up more of the bed than when he was stretched out with his long tail and claws extended. He never should have let the pangolin share the bed with him, but now, after all these years, it was too late. Percy wouldn't sleep anywhere but at Abel's feet.

He tried to nudge the sleeping ball off, but the only thing harder than moving a sleeping pangolin was moving an awake pangolin, and he didn't want to risk waking Percy. So he slipped his feet out from underneath the snoring ball of scales and sat with his knees pulled up to his chest. He rested his chin on his knees and yawned again.

It was still 11:57. Why did waiting for something always make time slow down?

He had the shades wide open so the glow from the billboards and the lane lights and the landing platforms filled his room. A cheerful ad for Firebreather Soda blinked from the roof across the way, soaking him in vibrant red and yellow light. He didn't need a flashlight to see his cards, and in three minutes, when the cleaning dragons came, it'd be bright as noon on a cloudless day.

Cleaning night happened six times a year, and in his entire thirteen years, Abel had never managed to stay awake for it even once. His mother insisted he was awake for it when he was a baby, because he was *always* awake when he was a baby, but he didn't think that counted. He couldn't remember and wouldn't have known what he was seeing anyway. Babies didn't know what dragons were and definitely didn't know what the Department of Sanitation was.

Now that he was thirteen, he knew. Every two months, all the buildings in the city put their big bales of garbage on the roof, and a team of long-wing Infernals flew over each neighborhood to burn up the trash with their fiery breath. Then a team of Goatmouth short-wing dragons followed and ate up all the ashes. The fire from the Infernals stayed overhead and couldn't hurt you unless you were standing on the roof of a skyscraper at midnight for some reason, but Goatmouth dragons would eat *anything* they saw: ashes or metal or food scraps . . . or pets. Or people.

In preschool, everyone watched a video about the dangers of being outside on cleaning nights, and they'd watched it at the start of every school year since. The video hadn't been updated since before Abel was born. He didn't know the star's name, though she'd been a famous actor when his parents were younger. She'd also famously lost her teenaged son when he snuck out on a cleaning night and got eaten by a Goatmouth.

That was not the kind of fame anyone wanted.

So it was a pretty big surprise when Abel looked out the window and saw a person in all black leaping across the balconies outside his building, with two minutes until midnight.

He looked up at the silhouettes of the dragons circling in a wide V formation, preparing for the big burn. Infernals were bright red from nose to tail, and they had the longest flame range of any dragon, but they flew slowly. The shadows of Goatmouths swarmed around them like flies around a light bulb. These "dragonflies" were fast as lightning when they dove and weighed five tons each. A Goatmouth dragon could swallow the small person leaping along the balconies without even slowing down to chew.

Ninety seconds left.

The Infernals made a wide turn, circling for their approach to Abel's neighborhood.

The figure outside scurried along a landing platform, midway up the next-door apartments. They ducked the security cameras and then leapt into open air, catching a balcony ledge on Abel's building with their fingertips, then hoisted themselves up.

Could it be a tagger? There was already a graffiti mural on this side of the building. Someone had painted a blazing sun, which held the silhouette of a roaring dragon inside it. It was the symbol of the Red Talons kin, the gang who ran this neighborhood. No one would dare tag over their symbol. Then again, no one would dare climb the side of his building on cleaning night with . . . oh no . . . only sixty seconds to go!

The figure didn't stop at the graffiti. Instead, they jumped like a dancer from one balcony railing to the next. They leapt fearlessly, and there was something familiar in their movements, something Abel couldn't quite place.

He looked up toward the cleaning dragons, just above the

skyline now. He saw the first hint of flame from their lips, and then, FWOOOSH!

The sky ignited. A wall of blazing orange fire filled his view from one end to the other, and spilled toward his building like a sheet being pulled over the neighborhood.

Twenty seconds.

He had to lean his head against the glass to see the figure now: scurrying from above, two stories up and three apartments over from his.

Why did they look so familiar?

It didn't matter. They were about to be burned to a crisp, or eaten by Goatmouths, or both.

Ten seconds.

Now the figure was just above his window. The dragons were across the street, flames nearly blue with heat as they incinerated the rooftop garbage around the Firebreather soda ad. The glass of his window warmed his forehead.

And then Percy uncurled at the foot the bed.

"Percy, what are you doing?"

Percy never uncurled for strangers.

And that's when the figure outside dropped down to Abel's window. The climber had on clawgloves, one of which held the window frame. Good thing too, as his room was on the sixty-seventh floor. The other pulled the mask off her face.

"Lina!" Abel shouted.

His sister clung by one hand to his windowsill, as the longwings lit the sky on fire.

Ashes rained into her dark hair, and two dozen ravenous dragons dove from above.

"OPEN THE WINDOW, PLEASE!" she shouted, although the roar and screech of the city's dragons directly above their building made her voice almost impossible to hear.

Abel knew what she was asking—because what *else* would she be asking?—but he was frozen in place. He was a little embarrassed his big sister was seeing him in his Dr. Drago boxer shorts playing with his DrakoTek cards, and he was *a lot* shocked to have seen her leaping from building to building at midnight.

He remembered the actor whose teenager had been eaten on cleaning night. Was this just something teenagers did, recklessly courting death and disaster? Now that he was a teenager, would he end up doing it too?

Unlikely. He didn't even like heights, which was how he'd failed his Dragon Rider Academy Entrance Exam when he was eleven and ended up at Municipal Junior High 1703.

"Um, like now, please?!" His sister pounded on the glass to make sure he understood.

"Right! Right!" Abel unlatched the window. Even in the face of great and imminent peril, he was easily distracted.

That was also why he'd failed his Dragon Rider Academy Entrance Exam. According to the report they got in the mail with his Notice of Failure, he was reckless, easily distracted, and afraid of heights. Not a great combo for a dragon rider. He really wished he hadn't seen the report. Sometimes it was better not to know what adults thought about you.

The moment he slid the window open, his sister tumbled into his room and slammed it shut behind her.

A huge claw swept over the window frame, screeching across the dragon-proof glass, backlit by the fire in the sky. It cast a huge claw-shaped shadow over Abel, his sister, and the wall of his bedroom.

It was 12:01 a.m.

All apartment buildings were made with Dragon-Resistant Materials, so they were safe inside. The claw vanished above the window frame, and Abel fell back onto his bed, trying to slow his heartbeat down by rubbing Percy's chin and taking deep breaths. Goatmouths were a lot bigger up close than he'd thought they'd be.

Military riders and Dragon's Eye agents flew dragons three times their size or more. Abel was relieved for a second that he *had* failed his Academy entrance exam. As much as he dreamed of being a dragon rider like his oldest brother, Silas, he was more likely to get a job at Chimera's All-Night Coffee + Comics like his sister. He loved comics and games and books, and he imagined he'd love coffee too, if he was ever allowed to try it.

Lina was supposed to be working the night shift at Chimera's right now.

Instead, she was in his room, catching her breath with her head between her knees. Her hands shook. He noticed that her black shirt was shredded at the shoulder but not torn. It looked . . . burned. His heart was racing, but it was his big sister who had been in grave peril a few seconds ago.

Abel turned to her. "UM. WHAT?" She looked up at him, and he asked, a little softer, "Are you okay?"

He felt weird, because she was his big sister and she was usually the one checking on him, but there was nothing usual happening right now. He *really* wanted to know what was going on. He also *really* wanted to put some pants on. He crossed to his dresser to throw on a pair of sweats.

Lina's dive into the room had scattered his DrakoTek cards across the floor. She looked over them and then up at his room like she was surprised to find herself there. Her eyes swept over his *KINWARS* movie posters, his Ravenous Riot album covers, and his fan art of half a dozen famous kin dragon riders.

The kin were gangsters. In real life, they weren't the sort of people he wanted anything to do with. Every neighborhood had its powerful kin. They hung out on street corners and in seedy clubs. They committed crimes and took money from honest people in exchange for protection from the other kins in other neighborhoods, who *also* committed crimes and took money from honest people in exchange for protection from the other kins . . . and so on. Every kin threatened people and every kin stole; it was just a question of who they threatened and who they stole from.

But the cool thing all kins did was battle with their dragons in epic street rumbles, which were the stuff of legends. Abel loved movies and comics about the kinners, even if they scared him in real life.

"They're not that good," Lina said about his drawings.

"Hey!" he objected. Instead of explaining what she was doing leaping across buildings when she should have been inside selling coffee and comic books to the weird customers who shopped at Chimera's on a Sunday at midnight, she was insulting his art.

"No, your drawings are great!" she apologized. "I meant those riders. The best dragon riders in a kin battle are the ones you never hear about. They never get caught. I'm just saying. You only ever hear about the losers."

Abel rolled his eyes. Lina was always correcting him about kin stuff, like she was some kind of expert. Some of the kinners from the Red Talons kin shopped at Chimera's, and so did members of the two other big kins in the city, the Sky Knights and the Thunder Wings. Chimera's was considered neutral territory, because it was the only good comic shop in the city and everyone liked Fitz, the owner. But selling kinners chocolate-covered espresso beans and the latest issue of *WingMaidens* didn't make Lina an expert in the city's criminal underworld.

"So . . . um . . . like . . . what were you doing outside? I didn't know you could parkour like that. It was . . ." What could he say? Scary? Bonkers? Stupid? "Cool," he said.

"It was *not* cool," Lina scolded him, and then pulled something out of her shirt. A comic. "It was a mistake. Something went wrong . . . I don't have time to explain. Just . . . this is for you."

She held the comic out to him. It was an issue of *Dr. Drago* he already had. Drago Khorram, famed vigilante veterinarian, helps an injured wyvern that belongs to a kin boss. The kin boss forces him to poison an enemy kin's dragon, but Drago won't defy his veterinarian's oath to do no harm, so his family gets kidnapped. He has to team up with Detective Stoneheart to rescue them.

Abel read it the day it came out.

"Thanks, but I have that one already," he told Lina.

"You don't have *this* one," she said. "There's variant artwork on page eighteen. *Trust me.* This one is rare."

He took it from her, and as he did, a small keycard fell out. It looked like the kind from a hotel, but when he picked it up, he saw it was blank. No logo even.

"Your bookmark?" He offered it back to her.

"Everything okay in there?" His mom knocked on his door.

Lina pressed herself up against the wall by Abel's dresser. She put her finger on her lips, imploring him to keep quiet about her.

He frowned, but he understood. There was a code between siblings that was like the code between kin: You don't snitch on your siblings.

"Yeah, Mom," he called through the door. "I was just staying up to see the cleaning."

"I heard talking," she called back. The knob turned. Lina's eyes widened.

"Don't come in!" Abel yelled. "I'm . . . uh . . . not dressed?"

The doorknob stopped turning. "Go to sleep, honey," his mom said, and he heard her steps as she went back to her bedroom.

"Thanks," Lina whispered.

"You need to tell me what's going on," Abel insisted.

"I can't," she said. Abel's shoulders tensed. She was in *his* room, and he'd protected her from the dragons outside *and* from their mom. She owed him an explanation. He was about to tell her so, when there was a loud knock at the door.

BOOM. BOOM. BOOM.

But it wasn't his door. It was the apartment door. Who would be visiting after midnight? And on cleaning night, when no one was supposed to be on the streets?

He looked out the window. The dragons had moved on from the neighborhood. There was no ash falling, so the Goatmouths would have left too.

BOOM. BOOM. BOOM.

"I need you to promise me something," Lina whispered.

"Are you going to tell me what's going on?"

"I need you to keep it safe," she said.

"Keep *what* safe?"

"Promise me," Lina repeated, desperate. "And you can't tell anyone I was here. Not Mom or Dad or Silas. Especially Silas. For all their safety."

"Who is at the door?" Abel asked. "Are they here for you?"

Instead of answering him, his sister grabbed his shoulders and bent to look him straight in the eyes. "Promise me," she said.

"I promise," Abel agreed.

"Swear on a secret," she pressed him.

"What?"

"So I know you'll keep you the promise you make, swear to me on your biggest secret," she said.

"I don't have any . . . I mean . . . I . . ." His heart was racing again, but his sister was looking at him with such intensity, in a way no one had ever looked at him before, like this was the most important thing in the world. She chewed her lip anxiously. She was his big sister and he loved her; how could he not do what she asked?

"I swear," he said quietly. "I swear on the secret that I . . . well . . . um . . ." He scratched the back of his neck. It felt hot. "I'm glad I failed the Academy entrance exam. I was, like . . . afraid to go."

He exhaled loudly. His neck cooled, like the heat of the secret had been released just in time.

His sister nodded. Then she even smiled. "I'm glad you failed it too, you know. But don't worry. I won't tell anyone. Your secret is safe with me."

"And yours with me," Abel felt confident, mature, like someone who could be trusted.

BOOM. BOOM. BOOM.

"We know you're home!" a loud voice shouted from the hall outside the apartment. Abel's new confidence faltered. "Open the door or we open it for you!"

He heard his parents' footsteps. He cracked his bedroom door open and could just see the apartment door if he leaned out a little. As his mom opened it, his father stood in the middle of the room, trying to look tough. He'd only recently gotten out of the hospital for Scaly Lung, and had lost a lot of weight, so his version of tough wasn't very intimidating. It looked even more ridiculous when two big enforcers from the Red Talons kin thundered into the apartment and slammed the door behind them, bolting it shut.

"Kinners!" Abel gasped, turning back to his sister . . . but she was gone. He rushed to the window but couldn't even see which direction she went.

"Where's your daughter?" one of the kinners bellowed. Abel locked the latch on his window again before he poked his head back into the hall.

"She's . . . she's not here," his mother said.

"That's what they said at the comic shop too," the other kinner snarled.

Each had the Red Talons symbol tattooed on his neck; they each wore red scaled leather jackets with black shirts below them, and each one had a huge dragon's talon tucked into his belt. One was bald except for a tuft of blue hair just above the center of his forehead, while the other had shaved his bright blond hair in swirling stripes. That one's arms were bigger than Abel's entire waist, and he was the one who crossed the living room to the shelf in the hall.

Abel pulled back and watched him through the crack in the door as he took a framed family picture off the shelf. He held it up.

"You have two other children," he said. "Silas and Abel, right?"

Abel couldn't see his parents now, but he could imagine their worried faces. He'd seen his parents' worried faces a lot: like when Mom got promoted to deputy shift supervisor at the dragon feed plant and knew she wouldn't be around to make sure Abel did his homework and ate healthy dinners. Or when Silas aced his Academy entrance exam and went off to be a cadet, and Lina aced *her* exam and *refused* become a cadet, and worked at the all-night comics and coffee shop instead. Abel had also seen their worried faces when he failed his entrance exam. He didn't need to see their faces to know what their faces were right now.

His parents had a lot to worry about.

They were about to have more.

"**How about we talk to** your other kids?" the blue-tufted kinner suggested.

"Relax, Grackle," the blond one said. "I'm sure these fine citizens will tell us where their daughter is before we have to involve their *innocent* children."

Abel didn't like the way the goon had said "innocent." It sounded like he was ordering something at a restaurant, something served bloody with its head still attached.

"Tell us where your daughter is," the one named Grackle said. "For your children's sake."

"If she's not at work, then . . ." His mother's voice trailed off.

"Enough!" the blond one shouted. He threw the family photo to the ground, then stomped the glass with his boot. "Grackle. Get the youngest."

"No!" his mom shouted, but Grackle was already stomping down the hall, shoving open doors. His father rushed forward, but the blond kinner clotheslined him with one arm, sending him gasping to the floor. If Abel's dad had a breath weapon like a dragon, it'd have been gasping.

Abel retreated to his bed so he could pretend to be asleep, which seemed a pretty pathetic defense, but he didn't have any other ideas. He heard Grackle slam open the bathroom door, then the closet, then Silas's old room, where he hadn't lived since going off to the Academy. The next door was Abel's, and it burst open so hard that it bounced shut in Grackle's face again.

"Ouch!" the kinner shouted, then opened it more gingerly.

Abel sat up in bed, acting like he'd just woken up, although he was still clutching Lina's comic to his chest.

"Rise and shine, kid," Grackle snarled at him. "Get out here."

Abel set the comic down under his blanket and followed the big man out to the living room.

"What's going on?" he pretended.

His mother had her fists balled. "If you hurt my son—" she said.

"No one's hurting anyone," the blond one said, which would have sounded more convincing if he didn't currently have one foot pinning Abel's father to the floor. "The young man's just going to tell us if he knows where his sister is."

"She's at work," Abel said.

The blond one frowned. Then, with one arm, he swept everything else off the shelf behind him: the books, the photos, the little glass dragon statues each of the kids had made in fifth-grade glassblowing class. Abel's hadn't looked much like a dragon, but he still hated to see it shatter.

Just then, Percy came charging from his room, all clattering claws and snorting snout. A pangolin was mostly harmless, unless they decided there were ants in your pants. Then their claws wouldn't stop tearing until they found them, or left nothing but shredded skin and broken bones.

"Call it off!" Grackle yelled. He let go of Abel and pulled the curved dragon's talon from his belt. Not much could get through a pangolin's thick scales, but a dragon's talon sure could.

"Percy, curl!" Abel commanded. Luckily, Percy listened, stopping his charge and rolling up into a defensive ball. Grackle looked like he might still attack, so Abel added an unnecessary "Stay!"

Grackle backed down, but instead of belting the talon, he touched it to Abel's neck. His dad gasped, though his mother's silence was sharper.

"Let me introduce myself." The blond one squatted down so his eyes were level with Abel's, while Grackle held him still. "My name is Sax." He tapped the image on his neck with two fingers. "Do you know what this tattoo means?"

Abel nodded. The man's breath smelled sour, and his teeth were stained a little green.

Abel had never looked this closely at a kinner before. The Red Talons were the biggest and most powerful kin in the city. They controlled his neighborhood and more than thirty others, and you could get a broken jaw by just looking at one of them wrong.

Abel had heard about a high schooler who drew a mustache on one of their symbols stenciled on a dumpster. In retaliation, the Red Talons made his girlfriend break up with him, then stole his clothes before dropping him off after curfew, naked, on the other side of the city. And that was just for making fun of their dumpster graffiti.

Adults who defied them got it a lot worse.

Abel wondered why they were looking for Lina. He feared it had something to do with the keycard and comic sitting under his blanket down the hall.

"You know it's not good to lie to us," Sax said. "Why don't you tell us where your sister is?"

"Like I said . . ." Abel did his best to sound nervous, which wasn't hard, because he was terrified. ". . . she's at work. She's gonna get me the new *Dr. Drago*."

"What was that you were reading when I came in?" Grackle snarled, and Abel's heart sank. He didn't think a kinner would've noticed. "Looked like the new one to me."

"Well . . ." Abel scrambled to think of something. Then he remembered the glassy look his parents got whenever he started talking about comics. "It wasn't the new, new one. There's a variant cover, you know? So, like, the story's the same but the artist accidentally drew Dr. Drago with a scar on his left hand, which he got from a steel wing that had a bad tooth in issue 441, but he doesn't have that scar anymore, because it got healed in issue 552 when he met with the Dragon King of Xiun, after he went on a quest to find the Ashen Ember of Tahir, which no one could actually find, because it was really just a metaphor for friendship or something. We're studying metaphors in a unit on literary devices in English class, but a lot of people don't think comics use literary devices, though as a visual medium, they totally do, so I think that we should get to read comics for school, and I also think that Dr. Drago—"

"Tongues of fire, boy, shut it!" Sax yelled, cutting him off. He shook his head and rubbed his jaw, looking at the mess on the floor. He turned away from Abel and spoke to Abel's mom. "Get a message to your daughter," he said. "Tell her she better show herself at the Half-Wing by Nocturn this time

Saturday. Tell her it's for her own safety . . ." He looked back at Abel, and then to Abel's dad on the floor. "And yours."

With that, he strolled out the door. Grackle followed, knocking an art poster off the wall. He paused and looked back at them. "And don't even think about calling the Dragon's Eye about this. You'll just make it harder on yourselves."

Then he slammed the door behind him so hard it knocked one more picture to the floor. What did these goons have against pictures?

After their footsteps faded down the hall, the elevator dinged and the apartment fell silent as a sleeping dragon's hoard.

Abel was barefoot and didn't dare move into the living room with all the broken glass lying around. His mother helped his father up, while speaking as calmly as she could.

"Abel, everything is going to be fine. But I think you should go back to bed now."

"But—" he started.

"Now, please," his mother said, and he knew from her tone this was not up for discussion.

The moment he was back in his room, he pressed his ear to the door and listened.

"I'm texting Silas," Mom said.

"But they told us not to—" Dad objected.

"He's our son," Mom replied. "He needs to know what's happening."

"But *we* don't even know what's happening," Dad said. "How did our Lina get mixed up with the Red Talons?"

"We don't know that she's mixed up with them."

"These kin think they can bully everyone. They've got some nerve coming here and—" A cough interrupted his dad, which then set off a fit of them. His Scaly Lung acting up.

"Go to bed, honey," Mom said. "I'll clean up. And Silas will come by tomorrow."

"I can't let you clean up all by your—" But he was cut short by another coughing fit. Pretty soon Abel heard his mom leading his dad back to their room.

He went to his own bed and pulled out the comic Lina had given him. He studied the blank keycard for a moment, though it told him nothing, then flipped to page eighteen. His shades were still open, so the flashing lights of the billboards and the red-and-green aerial lane markers let him see well enough. He studied each panel, looking for the variant Lina had said he'd find.

He didn't notice it at first and might not have noticed it at all, except the billboard across the way changed to an extra-bright ad for Long-Wing Cruises summer vacation sale to the Glass Sea, starting at only $1,878 a person. As if any family in this neighborhood had that much money to spend on a dragonback cruise.

With the glow off the ad's smiling faces and gleaming glass vistas, Abel was able to see something strange in the third panel on the page. On a hand-painted sign in the background of the scene, there was an address inked in tiny letters, and the handwriting was definitely his sister's.

Keep it safe, she had said. Maybe she hadn't meant the comic or the keycard. Maybe she'd meant whatever was at that address. He didn't know where in the city it was. He'd have to look it up tomorrow when his mom unlocked his phone again—*if* she unlocked his phone again.

As he lay back in bed, he stared up at the night sky, where his sister had so recently been scaling skyscrapers. He decided to think this through until he figured out what was going on, even if he had to stay up all night to do it.

So of course, the next thing he knew, it was morning.

He'd fallen asleep and dreamed about kin battles, and his sister leaping between skyscrapers, and goons kidnapping his parents. When he opened his eyes, he heard his brother's voice in the living room, and Silas did not sound happy at all.

SILAS NEVER SOUNDED THAT HAPPY to begin with, but when Abel came out of his room in the morning, his brother was practically fuming. He stood in the kitchen in his cadet's uniform, wagging his index finger at his parents like they were teens who'd stayed out past curfew.

Mom and Dad were seated at the kitchen table, staring at their hands. They looked so small, wearing their pajamas while Silas had on the dark green coat and silver pants of the dragon cadets.

"First of all, you should never have let Lina work at a place like Chimera's," he scolded them. "And definitely not on the night shift! It's a gathering place for criminals, radicals, and ne'er-do-wells!"

What kind of nineteen-year-old calls people "ne'er-do-wells"? Abel wondered.

"You know Lina needed to get a job after . . ." His mother paused. "Last year," she said, but the damage was already done. They all knew what she really meant was *after your dad got sick and stopped working and we almost lost our apartment.* Dad studied his fingers on the table, shame flapping around him with invisible wings. He looked like he wanted to be anywhere else in the world but at that table.

Abel cleared his throat, and all three heads turned toward him. "Hey, Silas," he said.

Silas frowned and didn't even greet him. "Shouldn't you get to school?"

"I don't have to leave yet," he said. "And I wanted to see you. How's training? Do you have a dragon? Have you flown out of the city? What are the Glass Flats like? Did you get aviator glasses? Can I see them?"

He hadn't meant to pepper his brother with questions, but once he'd started, he couldn't stop. Silas was the only person he knew who actually got to fly battle-grade dragons, and Abel just *had* to hear what it was like. He was so excited, he'd almost forgotten about the kinners who trashed their apartment and the keycard Lina had left in his care. When he remembered, he had to fix his face so he didn't give anything away. She'd told him *especially* not to tell Silas.

"What are you doing?" Silas grumbled at him. "You look like you have to drop a dragon's egg."

"Silas!" their mom scolded.

"What?" Silas shrugged.

"You may talk like that at the Academy, but we use our manners in this house," their dad said.

Apparently, Abel's "keeping secrets" face looked a lot like Abel's "ate too many Firechips and needs to use the bathroom" face.

"Sorry, I forget how *sensitive* Abel is," Silas said sarcastically as he brushed the bangs off his face. All dragon cadets had the sides and back of their heads shaved and their hair long on top. Abel thought it was the coolest look, but somehow Silas wore it like an insult aimed right at his little brother. They both knew Abel had failed the same exam that Silas had aced. The knowledge burned the air between them. "Look, I shouldn't even be here," Silas said. "The only reason my commanding officer gave me leave to visit is because my wyvern needed the exercise and—"

"You have a wyvern!?" Abel blurted. "Does it have a breath weapon? Do you get wing blades? Speed boosters? A bomber harness? What do you feed it?" He couldn't help his curiosity, though it withered under the glare Silas fixed on him.

"That's classified," he said. "And I'm not here because you're a dragon fanboy," he added. "I'm here because Lina is in trouble."

"Can you help her?" Dad asked. "She's your sister, and family is more important than any uniform you wear."

"The uniform isn't just an outfit," he said. "It is a statement of values and of my oath to serve the laws of Drakopolis."

"Of course it is," their father said. "And you do look spiffy in it; I just meant—"

"I don't look *spiffy*!" Silas objected, his voice cracking. "This uniform is a sacred trust with the leaders of our city to protect and enforce our way of life."

"Okay, fine . . ." their father said. "It's a sacred trust, not spiffy at all. So can you use that sacred trust to help your sister? Or is it only that you help the law, the law doesn't help you?"

For a moment, Silas looked like a kid again, when he still lived in the apartment and woke up early on weekends to play DrakoTek with Abel on the living room floor. Then he set his jaw and tried to look tough. He even lowered his voice so it sounded deeper than normal.

"Careful, Dad," he nearly snarled. "That's dangerous talk."

"One of my children is already in danger," Dad answered back. He and Silas had a way of getting under each other's skin whenever they talked, ever since Silas went to the Academy. Their father had not supported the decision.

"Lina has more than some kinners to worry about," Silas said. His voice took on the flat tone they must teach at Dragon Rider Academy. "I'm sorry to tell you, but your beloved daughter—"

"She's your sister, Silas," their mom interrupted, but Silas ignored her.

"Your beloved daughter," he repeated, "is a well-known dragon thief. And from the files I've seen, she was bound to cross the wrong kin eventually."

"No . . ." Dad whispered. Silas reached into his green coat and pulled out his phone. He swiped up and showed them photos on the screen, so Abel had to cross into the kitchen and lean over their shoulders to see.

It was Lina, in the same black outfit she'd worn in his room. But it wasn't burned yet, and she was inside some very fancy-looking stables, with beautiful glass sculptures set into niches between iron doors.

Silas swiped over to a video, and Abel watched, holding his breath, as Lina hacked into the keypad next to the door. A green light blinked, and she slipped inside. The video cut to a huge room . . . a dragon's stall. They could only see the edge of a wing lying across the floor before Lina threw something at the camera, blackening the lens.

Silas took the phone away.

"She breaks into stables in the Golden District and steals valuable dragons. We suspect she works for the Sky Knights kin."

"Lina's in a kin?!" Abel gasped.

The Sky Knights were the second-biggest kin in the city. Rumors said their leader was a former military captain who ran it like a private army. They were criminals just like the Red Talons, but they were known for their discipline and loyalty. Red Talons fought and betrayed each other all the time, but Sky Knights never turned against their own. They were merciless against anyone who tried. Abel couldn't picture his sister as a Sky Knight.

"You need to stay away from Lina," Silas told Abel, tucking his phone back into his coat and straightening his collar, even though it was already straight. He puffed up his chest. "*All* of you need to stay away from her. The Sky Knights are dangerous."

"But what do we do about the Red Talons?" Abel demanded. "They're dangerous too. Or do you not care anymore because you're a fancy dragon cadet?"

"Abel, please," their mother scolded him, but he didn't care.

Silas was acting like he was so much better than them, like he didn't need a family because he had a uniform. Abel was sick of it. Silas hadn't even called home on his birthday, and he'd seen how that made his parents cry. He wanted his big brother to apologize, to help them, instead of being such a . . . such a . . .

"You're such a fart rider!" he yelled, which wasn't the best insult, but it was the best he could think of in the moment. He knew he couldn't win a fight with Silas, but that didn't mean he couldn't *pick* a fight. If Silas was arguing with him, then his brother would be distracted from saying anything else about Lina. And the less Silas told their parents about Lina, the better. "They should train you at the Fart Academy; you'd be a top student!"

His mother sighed, and Silas just shook his head.

"Grow up, Abel," he grumbled, and turned to leave.

"Will you be back for Saint George's Day?" Dad asked him.

"I don't know, Dad," said Silas. "It depends on the Academy. I've got a lot of work to do."

Their dad looked like a deflating balloon as Silas opened the apartment door. Abel's brother stopped halfway through and turned back. Abel perked up. Was he about to apologize? To make Dad smile or tell Abel something cool about his wyvern?

"If any of you know Lina's whereabouts, report them to the local office of the Dragon's Eye *immediately*," he said. He paused, then added, "For her own safety," and he shut the door with one curt nod.

Abel's parents sat at the table, stunned by the revelation that their middle child was in a dangerous kin being hunted by *another* dangerous kin, *and* by the city's secret police.

Silas's last words echoed in Abel's head. *For her own safety.* The Red Talons had said the same thing. Lina had said it too, when she made Abel swear to keep her secret. He was beginning to think that no one used that phrase to say what they meant. Was he the *only* one who was actually worried about his sister's safety?

He had to go to the address in the comic, but he'd need help first. An ally. Someone who would keep a secret without even needing to swear on it.

He needed his best friend, Roa.

They'd know what to do, and even if they didn't, they'd help him figure it out. It was, he felt, a good thing to have a best friend who was smarter than you were, even if they always won your DrakoTek cards.

"Time for school," his mother told him, pulling his lunch box out of the fridge. When had she had time to make him lunch? "Get dressed quickly, please."

He didn't need to be told twice. He threw on his white shirt, a pair of black jeans that were clean enough, and his green school hoodie that probably wasn't. Then he grabbed his school tie off the dresser without putting it on and snatched the lunch from the table on his way out.

"Hey!" his dad objected. Abel came back, gave both his parents quick hugs, and ran for the elevators. The landing platform was on the ninety-eighth floor, and he arrived just in time to see the school bus pull up its bridge and flap away.

"WAIT!" ABEL SHOUTED, WIND WHIPPING his hair.

The parents of younger children who'd come to put their kids on the bus looked at him with pity. The walls in their building weren't thick; surely everyone knew by now that his family had been visited by the Red Talons kin last night. He recognized Ms. Deloggia from downstairs, who had twins in third grade, and Maddie's dads from the preschool, and Auntie Novick, who was definitely an informant for the Dragon's Eye. When they saw him looking at them, they all looked away.

The huge Red-Bearded Long-Wing with the bus strapped to its back had lifted high above the platform to move to the next building, but the attendant leaned over the side and shook his head at Abel.

"Late again?" he shouted down. "It's only Monday!"

Abel opened his arms wide, pleading. This was not the first time he'd been late for the bus this school year. It wasn't the fifth time or the twelfth time or the thirtieth time either. He was late for the bus *a lot*.

The attendant whistled to the pilot, who sat in a harness just behind the huge dragon's horns, holding the complicated steering rig. The pilot glanced down, morning sun catching the light on his aviator glasses. He eased the dragon over the platform.

The attendant dropped a knotted climbing rope and waved Abel up. Most kids got to walk across the boarding bridge while the dragon hovered right in front of the platform, but the pilot wasn't about to lower and steady a fifteen-ton dragon again just for Abel. He had about five seconds to grab the rope before it flew off. He'd have to beg his mom for taxi fare that she knew he'd promise to repay and never, ever would.

He slung his backpack over his shoulder and climbed the rope as quickly as he could, feeling the dragon lurch. Abel looked down as the building dropped away. The deep chasm of the city street opened below. In this neighborhood, even the smallest apartment building was at least a hundred stories high . . . and his was not the smallest one.

Below his sneakers, medium-wing taxis and delivery dragons zipped to and fro between the hovering lane makers at different heights. Bus-backed long-wings glided along side streets, heading for platforms and landing pads. Above him, long-haul freighters towed by Gray-Banded Cloud Scrapers, Red Dracarios, and Green Goliaths moved the morning's deliveries every which way. It always amazed Abel how life in the bustling city went on and on, indifferent to whatever epic dramas were playing out in his own life—whether it was his father in the hospital, his brother shipping out for the Academy, or now, his whole family in serious trouble with the kin. Drakopolis never stopped moving.

Once he was on board the bus, the attendant hauled the rope up and grumbled at him. "At least you'll have strong arms by the end of the school year."

"Thanks for the rope," Abel grumbled back, and weaved his way deeper into the crowd of kids, looking for an open seat. The straps that held the passenger compartment on the dragon's back creaked and groaned. He sat down near the back and watched the graffiti change as they made their stops, the spray-painted symbols forming an unofficial map of the city's neighborhoods.

After a few minutes flying, the Red Talons' dragon-sun symbol gave way to the Sky Knights' infinity dragon—an armored infinity symbol with the head of a dragon devouring its own tail. It was stenciled across walls and billboards, on the ledges of buildings, and across boarded-up apartment windows. Abel shuddered at it, thinking of Lina, wondering how she could keep this secret from him.

He hoped she was still okay. The Sky Knights were the only kin who organized attacks against the government, which might make them more dangerous than even the Red Talons. At least the Red Talons were just greedy. The Sky Knights were greedy *and* political. They had more members in Windlee Prison than any other kin.

What if his sister ended up there too? Bad things happened in Windlee. Exile would be more merciful.

Soon, they left Sky Knights territory, and he saw a lightning bolt with a dragon's head sprayed across a billboard for the LongTooth Retirement Complex. He was in Thunder Wings territory now, which meant Roa's neighborhood.

The Thunder Wings were the smallest of the Big Three kins, but they were also the smartest—into science and invention. Their goons didn't usually rob people with brute force, they just hacked into their bank accounts and stole from them online. They bred illegal dragons and built illegal weapons and sold illegal medicines, some of which didn't even work. Being smart didn't make them honest. Also, being smart didn't make them any less scary. They used violence when they needed to. You didn't last long as kin in Drakopolis without a bloody battle or two, and you didn't control entire neighborhoods *just* by being smart.

After three more stops in Thunder Wings territory, Roa got on and made their way through the overcrowded bus to find Abel.

"You need help with your tie?" they asked, plopping down beside him on the bench.

Abel nodded. Roa swiped the tie off his neck, wrapped it around their own, then tied it into a loose but tidy knot. They pulled it over their head and gave it back to him to put on.

"Thanks," he said, glad to have a friend who knew as much about their school uniform as they did about the care and maintenance of dragons, both in DrakoTek and in real life.

Roa's parents sent them to after-school veterinary classes at the community college three days a week. They'd have gone five days a week if they were allowed to, but the college said a seventh grader shouldn't spend *that* much time making all their adult classmates look bad. Roa was a certified genius. Abel couldn't imagine how they had flunked the Academy entrance exam, but that was one subject they never spoke about. Otherwise, they told each other *everything*.

"You really need to learn how to tie that yourself," Roa told him.

"But then what would I need you for?" he joked.

Roa had changed their hair again, spiking it and dyeing the barbs a deep, jammy purple that alternated with bleached blond.

Abel was always amazed that their parents let them do that. If he'd ever tried to dye his hair, his mom would've killed him. Roa had tried to give him a green streak once, but his hair was so dark it didn't show up enough to get him in trouble. Roa's parents were cool like that, though. They didn't even blink when Roa told them they were gender nonbinary, meaning they didn't identify as a boy or a girl, and that their preferred pronouns were "they" and "them." It had taken Abel longer to get it right than it had Roa's parents. He still felt bad about all the times in elementary school he'd used pronouns that made Roa feel wrong, but Roa shrugged it off.

"You know better now," they always said. "That's what matters."

Abel tucked the tie into his hoodie and wiped his palms on his jeans. Roa was wearing magenta jeans, because the school uniform instructed that all students had to wear pants or skirts and a white shirt with a tie, but it didn't say the pants had to be boring. Some days Roa wore a plaid skirt covered in spray paint; some days Roa wore jeans and suspenders. Some days Roa used their tie as a belt. The rules didn't say they had to wear the tie on their neck. Roa knew all the rules and every way to stretch them.

It helped that they got straight As.

Abel, with his mediocre grades and i.e., much-less-chill parents, didn't have as much room to stretch the rules.

"I'm serious about the tie," Roa said. "Knowing all kinds of knots is important for more than tying neckties. You need to know knots to care for dragons too."

Abel shrugged. "When am I ever going to care for a dragon?" he said.

"Don't say that."

"I wasn't hunting for a compliment," he told them, a little irritably. Probably because he was tired. "Just that my grades at our sad school aren't even good. The best I can hope for is, like, working at a feed plant like Mom or repairing bus harnesses or something. They don't let losers like me *near* a dragon, at least not a cool one."

Okay, maybe he *was* hunting for a compliment. Silas had made him feel bad about himself.

Instead, Roa just took his hand and held it. That was better than anything they could've said to him. Sometimes, when he was worried or down on himself, his friend knew what he needed better than he did.

"I have something to tell you," he whispered, then looked around the packed bus. Outside, the long-wing had caught a breeze and risen above the buildings to glide the rest of the way to school. The traffic sounds of honking and roaring and flapping had faded away. Abel could hear snippets of a half dozen conversations.

"—I beat level twenty-seven in one try!"

"Did not!"

"—Red Talons kin burned his face off—"

"Did not!"

"—sister got soda stuck in her ear because I dared her to laugh while chugging."

"Did not!"

"I can't tell you here," Abel said. "It's mega secret." In the city, even kids could be informers for the Dragon's Eye or for one of the kins. He'd seen a kin tattoo on an eighth grader once, though Roa told him it was probably just a temporary tattoo from a vending machine.

"Mega secret?" Roa said. "Paranoid much?"

"Yes," he answered. Abel closed his eyes to get a little rest before they got to school and also to keep himself from blurting out his sister's secret on the bus. He wasn't actually any good at keeping secrets. The longer he talked to Roa, the more likely it was he'd say it when other people could hear. Safer to sleep.

It felt like no time at all had passed when his stomach lurched up into his throat and the dragon bus dove for the school's landing platform. Out the window, three other dragon buses dove in unison, tucking their wings for speed, then spreading them wide within inches of each other and landing with a soft thud in a neat row.

Kids scrambled for the exits, down the dragon's wings. The attendant had to shout, like they did every morning, "Let the little ones off first! No trampling!"

As Abel stepped past him, the attendant grabbed his shoulder and leaned down.

"You tell your sister," he whispered. "Turn up at the Half-Wing, or else." He flashed his wrist in front of Abel to show him the dragon-sun tattoo of the Red Talons kin; then he gave Abel a less-than-gentle shove down the ramp.

"Was that a Red Talons tag?" Roa whispered as they headed for the door at the end of the platform. The school was only four stories high, but it was at the top of a ninety-story building, so their platform had guardrails and teachers all along it to keep the little kids from falling. Roa lowered their voice so the teachers couldn't hear. "I knew it. I knew that attendant was no good. What'd he want with you?"

"I'll . . . uh . . . tell you later," Abel said.

"You better," Roa replied, frowning at him. "Secrets between friends are like dragon bile."

It was Abel's turn to frown at Roa. They often forgot that Abel was not an expert in dragon biology.

"Dragon bile melts chemical bonds," Roa explained. "Like secrets melt friendships."

"Oh," Abel said sadly, although he wasn't worried about their friendship. He was going to tell Roa everything. He was thinking about his parents.

He wondered if secrets could melt families too.

6

"**AND WHAT ARE THE MEAL-TYPE** classifications of the order Dragonia?" Instructor Ally asked the class.

Beside Abel, Roa rolled their eyes, groaned quietly, and raised their hand.

"Anyone else?" Instructor Ally said. "Maybe someone I haven't called on four times already this morning?"

The rest of the class lowered their eyes. The instructor looked disappointed as she pointed at Roa. "Yes. Fine. Roa . . . *again.*"

"Charivores, whose meat must be served charred; rawivores, whose meat must be raw; vivivores, whose food must be eaten alive; pescatory dragons, who only eat fish; and herbivores, who eat vegetables. Oh, and freekavores, who only eat—"

"Freaks like you," Topher Agnew grunted from the corner. His buddies all laughed, though Roa acted like they didn't hear.

"Grains," Roa continued, undaunted by the bullies.

"Thank you, Roa," said Instructor Ally. "And, Topher, is your mother still out of work?"

"Uh, yeah," Topher growled, picking at his fingernails.

"Thought so," said Instructor Ally. "If you're going to make fun of someone in *my* class, you might consider that you have yet to pass a single test and are more useful to your family as dragon food than as a student."

"OOOO," the class cooed. Topher turned as red as the dragon who'd carried them to school.

"But . . . you're not supposed to say that!" Topher objected.

"I've never been good at doing what I'm supposed to." Instructor Ally grinned and rolled up her sleeves, showing arms that were covered in tattoos from elbow to wrist. There were colorful dragons wrapped around skyscrapers, rough outlines of claws and wings, and Abel thought he saw a kin tattoo also, the dragon-headed lightning bolt of the Thunder Wings. Instructor Ally had been a kinner in her youth. She even went to jail for it, before getting released and turning her life around to become a teacher. She never talked about it, but everyone knew the story. All the smart students were at least a little afraid of her.

Topher was not very smart.

"But they're such a show-off!" Topher pointed at Roa.

"If you can't treat your classmates with respect, then perhaps you don't want to be a part of this class. You can leave right now, or you can be a thoughtful member of our community. Your choice."

Topher balked and lowered his head. "Sorry, Roa," he grumbled.

Roa shrugged. They didn't have to accept his half-hearted apology and didn't intend to.

"If any of you find yourselves gainfully employed in dragon stables, you'll need to be mindful of the food classifications. They're not always obvious." Ally went on with the lesson. "There are long-wings that only eat grains, and there are tiny wingless ground dragons that will only eat live prey. Offer a dragon the wrong meal and what happens?"

Roa's hand shot up.

"Anyone else?" Instructor Ally tried.

When no one else raised their hand, Roa called out, "You get eaten!"

"Okay," the instructor announced. "To the locker rooms. Time to change for BDC."

As the class stood to go to Basic Dragon Care, she added, "Protective goggles are a *must* today. Our class has gone a whole month without a serious injury, and I'd like to keep that streak going for the remainder of the school year!"

· · ·

Thirty NERDs spread out over the gym, screeching and squawking and bumping into each other.

"Remember, identify the pack leader and you can control the herd!" Instructor Ally shouted over the din. "Group One, go!"

Abel and Roa stood next to each other in a line on the wall. They were in Group Two, so they had some time before their turn rushing into a pack of giant lizards and trying to corral them all into the big red square painted on the gym floor.

The NERDs were Educational Resource Dragons, officially called ERDs, though the kids all called them *not*-Educational Resource Dragons—NERDs. It was a label that had been around longer than Abel had been alive. They were bred specifically for schools by a company that everyone suspected was a secret front for the Thunder Wings kin. It made its money by charging a lot more for the NERDs than they actually cost to raise. Abel didn't think a kin would spend its time doing something so *boring* when they had real dragons to battle, but Abel didn't have a criminal mind. Not like his sister.

The thought gnawed at him. *Lina. A dragon thief.*

Even though teachers tried to convince the kids that the NERDs were real dragons, they never had much luck. NERDs were one-ton flightless lizards a little taller than an average adult. They had no breath weapons and only blunt teeth for eating leaves. They did have long tails and sharp claws that could do plenty of damage to a distracted seventh grader, though. Topher was in Group One, and Abel had to stifle a laugh when one of the tails swung around and nearly took his head off.

"Use your observation skills!" Instructor Ally shouted into the scrum of frantic Group One kids in their silver gym shorts and shirts. They all had loops of red fabric over their shoulders, which they were supposed to lasso around the NERDs' necks. Instead, they chased and dodged the miniature dragons, with no obvious success getting them to do anything but scatter around the gym. "They imitate the pack leader, the alpha dragon! Look for the signs of an alpha!"

"They all look the same!" Beni Gloss shouted. Abel had always liked Beni. Her older sister had been Lina's best friend until tenth grade, when she was arrested for protesting against the City Council. She was sent off to a labor camp for delinquent teens in some distant corner of the city. Beni worked hard to stay out of trouble and do well in school so that her family wouldn't be even more embarrassed, but she just wasn't that great a student. A NERD nearly trampled her.

"They don't all act the same!" Roa shouted at Beni, trying to help.

"Roa!" the instructor shouted. "Please let Group One do their own work. You'll get your turn."

Roa glared at their teacher, then leaned against the wall, crossing their arms. "So," they said to Abel. "You going to tell me your 'mega secret'?"

"Yeah, but you can't tell *anyone*," he said. "Swear."

"Who would I tell?" Roa asked.

"Swear," Abel repeated. "Swear on a secret."

Roa sighed and said, "Okay. I swear on that time I let you copy my math homework. I won't tell anyone."

Abel nodded and looked around, making sure no one else was listening to them. He leaned close to whisper.

He told Roa all about what happened last night, from the moment he first saw the figure in black scaling the buildings, to the moment this morning that Silas slammed the door on his family.

"Whoa," Roa said.

"Yeah," Abel agreed.

"The Red Talons are bad news," Roa added. "Sky Knights too."

"I know. I can't believe Lina's a Sky Knight and didn't tell me," Abel said.

"You can't believe she's in a kin or you can't believe she didn't tell you?"

"Both, I guess."

Roa thought about it. "It doesn't mean Lina doesn't love you that she didn't tell you. Maybe it was for your own safety."

"People keep using that phrase," Abel said. "I think they just say it as an excuse to make themselves feel better about being shady. Like you said, secrets are like dragon bile. They stink."

"I didn't say dragon bile stinks!"

"I mean, it's true, though, right? I bet dragon bile *does* stink!"

Roa laughed. Together they watched as Topher tried to tackle one of the NERDs, clearly thinking it was the alpha. He missed and almost got trampled by two others.

"Use your brains before you use your bodies!" Instructor Ally yelled. "You don't need to act like a NERD to catch one!" The whole class burst out laughing. "I meant ERD," she corrected herself.

"So, we're going to the address in the comic Lina gave you, right?" Roa said.

Abel was glad they'd offered to come along without him asking. He didn't want to go alone, but he didn't want to seem afraid to either. "We?" he said.

"Of course 'we'!" Roa said. "You need me. For your own safety." Abel did feel a lot safer with his best friend at his side. "WW3D," they added, which was a code they used whenever one of them was feeling nervous about something.

It meant "What would Dr. Drago do?" Abel and Roa figured, if you weren't feeling brave, better to borrow bravery from one of your heroes than run and hide. It was easier said than done.

But once it was said, there was no backing down. "WW3D," Abel repeated.

"Group One! Terrible job!" Instructor Ally called down from the catwalk above the gym. "To the wall. Group Two! You're up! Please show me something that won't make me give the whole class a pop quiz on Basic Observation!"

Everybody groaned, then looked to Roa. Now that they needed his best friend's skills, everyone who'd laughed at them before would do whatever Roa said without snark or hesitation. Nobody wanted a pop quiz on BO.

7

GROUP TWO STEPPED OFF THE wall in a straight line; then Roa took a couple steps in front of them. Abel stayed back with the rest of the line. He looked down at his knobby knees and up at the NERDs running amok. Their knees were bigger than his skull. Being so close to a herd of them raised chilly bumps up and down his arms.

"GURAWK!" one of the nearest NERDs squawked as it ran past, bumping into another one and tripping on its tail.

"We can rule that one out," Roa said. They ordered a red-headed kid named Bo to keep an eye on its position. "Let me know right away if it imitates any of the other ERDs."

Unlike their classmates, Roa never referred to the Educational Resource Dragons as NERDs. They had nothing but respect for *all* dragons, even the dumbest, most annoying school dragons, who couldn't shoot anything cool from their mouths or even fly.

"Ep ep!" Bo responded, and everyone rolled their eyes.

"Ep ep" was the unofficial Dragon Rider battle cry that cadets used to mean everything from "Yes, sir!" to "Excuse me, the dragon has lit my hair on fire." Bo had three older siblings, all of whom had graduated from the Academy, and two younger ones who were there now. He was the only sibling who hadn't gotten in, but he still used all the cadet slang. Everyone thought it was annoying, but Abel secretly understood why he did it.

It was hard to give up on a dream, even when the whole world made it very clear your dream wasn't going to come true.

Abel would never ride a battle dragon either.

"Remember your OODA loops!" Ally shouted at them all.

"Oo-dah??" Tall Andi asked.

Short Andi stood right next to her by accident. Usually, those two avoided being so close together. They hadn't exactly chosen their own nicknames. "That doesn't mean anything!"

"*Everything* means *something*," their teacher replied. When she didn't explain further, the group looked to Roa.

"Observe, orient, decide, act," Roa said. "In any situation, first you *observe*, then you *orient* yourself in the space, and *decide* what course of action to take, then *act* on it. OODA. It's what dragon cadets learn on day one."

"But . . . we're not dragon cadets," Short Andi said, looking at his sneakers.

"Skills are skills," Roa replied. "We don't need to pass some test to use them. We're just as capable as any greencoats."

Roa's encouragement made Short Andi smile. In truth, it made Abel feel a little better too.

"Observe the pattern of the ERDs' behavior," Roa said. "They're running in figure eights. See?"

Abel scanned the herd and saw that they were right. Some of the figure eights the dragons ran in were smaller than others, some went the length of the room and some the width, and some even went in opposite directions. It looked like chaos, but it wasn't, once you saw the pattern.

"That one!" Roa pointed. Abel followed their finger toward one of the NERDs who had swerved from the figure eight and was now running in a circle. The other dragons near it copied, and soon every dragon was running in circles. The loops were different sizes and going in different directions and intersecting with each other, just like with the figure eights.

"If you think you've got the alpha," their teacher called, "tag it!"

Roa adjusted their feet, orienting themselves in the space, then pulled the loop of red fabric off their shoulder. It was weighted on one end, and it had a small battery inside. When it was looped onto a NERD, it could be activated by the teacher's remote, delivering a small shock that would stun the dragon. If it really was the alpha, all the other NERDs would stop too. All they had to do was toss it over the dragon's neck, but Roa hesitated.

"You got this," Abel encouraged them. "Time to act."

Roa didn't move. "It's cruel," they said.

"The shock isn't painful," Abel reminded them. "Just startling."

"They say that, but there's a reason they don't let us control the battery, right?" Roa replied. "Because they know we'd shock each other and it would hurt!"

"Dragons are different," Abel said. "They're tougher."

"That doesn't mean we should be allowed to hurt them."

"I got it!" Prentiss Patek shouted, and raced from behind Roa into the throng of wingless dragons, tossing their fabric over the neck of the one Roa had pointed out. They missed and had to dive out of the way and scramble to safety against the opposite wall.

"Guess they don't got it," Topher giggled from the Group One line.

"I'll do it," Abel announced, hearing his heartbeat in his ears as he unlooped the fabric over his shoulders. He stepped forward. "You don't want to fail, do you? We'll have to take a BO quiz."

"I don't mind written quizzes," Roa said. "I *mind* hurting dragons."

"It won't hurt," Abel reassured his friend. "I promise."

He tracked the NERD with his eyes, watching it run in faster and faster circles. For a second, he thought it looked right at him. Then it bolted in another direction, which made all the others run the opposite direction too. Abel was about to get trampled!

"Ack!" he shouted, with a ridiculous crack in his voice that would've been embarrassing if he hadn't also thought he was about to die. He tossed the red fabric as he shouted and dove for the safety of the wall, covering his head with his hands in the same instant and only looking up again when he was clear.

If this were one of his comics, he'd have managed to land the fabric right around the alpha dragon's neck, through luck or some kind of skill he didn't know he had. A skill that would become useful later when he needed to be a hero.

But this wasn't one of his comics. Abel had missed by even more than Prentiss had, and now his fabric was being trampled by the entire scurrying herd of NERDs.

"Are you really going to make Roa do *everything* for you?" Instructor Ally yelled over the din. "Surely one of you is even a little capable? Are we going to need to practice hoops and pegs too, like we're in first grade? Because I did *not* become a teacher just to babysit a bunch of mucus-covered kids!"

"No, the *court* made you become a teacher to get out of Windlee Prison," Topher muttered.

"WHAT DID YOU SAY TO ME?" Instructor Ally roared at him. Abel wondered how in the flaming sky she'd heard Topher, though he was glad to see the bully's color turn from sickly white to dragon's breath red.

"I—I—" Topher stammered, not so brave now. Like most bullies, he wilted whenever someone stood up to him. "Nothing." He studied the floor between his sneakers.

"You and I are going to talk about your attitude . . . *in detention*," Instructor Ally told him. "And as for the rest of you sorry students, *we* are going to do drills for the rest of the—"

She was interrupted by an alarm blaring over the school speakers.

"Lockdown! Lockdown!" the principal's voice crackled. "Code Seven."

The automatic bars over the gym doors and windows snapped shut.

"What's Code Seven?" Abel asked Roa, who'd studied the school's student manual *and* a pirated version of the teacher's manual. They even knew all their teachers' salaries.

"Out-of-control dragons," Roa replied. Every kid turned to look through the bars and the glass outside the gym door . . . every kid except Roa.

"I don't see anything," Abel said, but then they heard screaming as a pack of NERDs chased an entire eighth-grade geometry class down the hall right past the gym doors. All the rooms were barred and locked, and the eighth graders couldn't get to safety.

"That's not supposed to happen," said Tall Andi.

"They're going to get trampled out there!" Short Andi cried out.

"Um," Roa said. "So are we . . . *in here!*"

Abel turned and saw the NERDs in the gym were no longer running in circles. They'd formed one long line with the alpha in the middle, their heads lowered like battering rams. Their eyes all rolled back, showing bright yellow from lid to lid, like egg yolks.

"That's *really* not supposed to happen," said Tall Andi.

Instructor Ally was too far away up on the catwalk to help. The dragons flexed their legs, readying a charge. They were about to crush Abel and his entire class into paste against the safety bars over the gym doors.

"This is not good," Abel said.

"All the NERDs have gone feral," Roa said. "This isn't natural."

They pointed up at the air vents in the gym, and Abel saw a purple gas pouring out.

"Something is *making* them do this," Roa said. They took the loop of fabric back off their shoulder, ready to toss it for real this time.

"Not worried about hurting a dragon anymore?" Abel asked.

"I'm trying to save them," Roa replied. Heavily armed Dragon Safety Officers flooded into the hallways outside the gym.

"And us, right?" Abel pleaded just as the scrum of dragons charged.

"GARUK!" THE ALPHA **NERD** BARKED.

The herd rushed forward. Roa stood their ground and tossed their loop of fabric around its neck. They looked up desperately to the catwalk, where Instructor Ally pushed the stun button. The battery fired, and the alpha screeched, grinding to a halt. The whole herd stopped with it.

Then the alpha roared and flung itself forward, the herd rumbling behind.

"Pheromones!" Roa shouted, as if that word would mean anything to Abel. He closed his eyes and braced himself for the impact of a dozen one-ton bodies covered in steel-hard scales slamming into his ninety-pound frame of fragile flesh. He'd be really bummed out if the last word he ever heard before dying was a word he didn't even know.

But there was no impact.

Instead, when he opened his eyes, Instructor Ally was on the back of the alpha dragon, both arms wrapped around its neck. She'd used Roa's fabric loop like reins to steer it away from the students. The other dragons followed. Even though they were only Educational Resource Dragons, not many people could leap from a catwalk onto the back of one and steer it off course mid-charge. Abel wondered if their instructor had been a dragon rider back in her kin days. Had she fought battles through the streets, dodging fire and ice, fleeing the Dragon's Eye and murderous kinners alike?

Had his teacher been . . . *awesome*?

"Climb!" Instructor Ally yelled back at the class.

The students began to scramble up the bars, to get as high off the ground as they could. Tall Andi's foot slipped, but Short Andi caught her. Abel's sweating hands had trouble gripping the bars. He dared a glance over his shoulder to where an out-of-control NERD growled, snapping its jaws at him.

He felt himself shoved out of the way, and the NERD bit the bar where he'd just been.

"Careful, dingus," Topher growled, and pulled him back to his feet. It was weird feeling to have your life saved and to get insulted by the same person simultaneously.

Just then, one of the side doors opened and a tactical squad of Dragon Safety Officers burst in. They had powerful stun sticks and body armor, and some kind of green spray that calmed the NERDs down.

As the spray misted the air, the big lizards sniffed, then purred, then leaned on each other, swaying half-asleep where they stood.

The siege was over.

The kids were sent back to their classroom in their sweaty gym clothes to wait for instructions. They had to walk single file, in silence, under the watchful eyes of the DSOs. The guards stood along the hall every ten feet with their weapons out, glaring at all the kids as they walked past. Down a corridor that one of the officers was blocking off, Abel saw a custodian scrubbing at a huge graffiti tag that covered the face of three lockers: a black-and-white stencil of a laughing dragon.

Abel stepped on Roa's heel in front of him, so that they glanced back. When they did, Abel bugged his eyes and nodded sideways to the tag.

"Wind Breakers," they said.

"Quiet!" one of the Dragon Safety Officers barked. The students marched the rest of the way back to their classroom in silence.

When Instructor Ally finally bustled in, she had a bandage on her forehead. "Principal Clayton has sent an alert to all your families. The school is closing early today so that cleanup and disinfection of the air ducts can begin." She paused. "The school will *also* be closed for the rest of the school term while a full investigation is conducted. You will be given remote learning assignments."

Some of the students cheered; some groaned. Roa looked downright stricken.

Instructor Ally shook her head and rolled her eyes, mouthing a silent word she probably thought her students didn't know. *Pheromones.*

They were seventh graders, though; they knew *all* the bad words. That made Abel wonder if "pheromones" was one of them.

"Psst," he whispered to Roa. "What's pheromones?"

They looked at him sideways, then back at their teacher. "Instructor Ally?" Roa asked. "What happened? Someone was pumping a purple gas through the vents. Was it pheromones? Was it the Wind Breakers kin?"

Their instructor nodded. "You're bound to hear about it on the news, so you might as well hear it from me. The authorities believe members of the Wind Breakers kin infiltrated the school and planted them in the air ducts."

"But what *are* pheromones?" Bo asked. Abel was relieved that he didn't have to.

"They're a chemical substance released into the environment by an animal, affecting the behavior or physiology of others of its species." Roa recited the definition. "Basically, they're animal mind-control smells."

"You mean the Wind Breakers wanted the NERDs to go crazy?" Topher wondered.

"That is the theory," Instructor Ally said without looking at him.

"*And* they got school canceled!" Topher cheered. "Go, Wind Breakers!"

"SHUT YOUR MOUTH, BOY!" Instructor Ally yelled, and Topher turned from mildly pinkish pale to practically white as printer paper. He pressed so far back into his seat he looked like he was on the back of a diving dragon. Their teacher calmed down, took a breath, and spoke quietly. "The Wind Breakers kin is a terrorist organization. As you know, it is against the law to express *any positive sentiment* about them. I am going to ignore your comment, Topher, as the ramblings of a scared little boy, and I will *not* report them to the authorities. But I don't want to hear another word out of you for the rest of the day, got it?"

"Got it," said Topher meekly.

"WHAT DID I JUST SAY?!" Instructor Ally thundered.

Topher looked like he was about to throw up. He nodded and tried desperately to keep his mouth shut. "While we're closed, you'll be serving detention with me," Instructor Ally added, and Topher nodded more.

Abel almost felt bad for the kid. Topher was the obvious kind of bully; he acted like a jerk because he was miserable. Everyone knew his brothers and sisters and cousins shared an apartment that was too small for all of them. He was the youngest, so he always got the last of everything and was always picked on at home. Everyone also knew that his mom had called the Dragon's Eye on a group of Thunder Wings who were robbing a pharmacy in their building. She lost her job because the Thunder Wings made her boss fire her. You didn't snitch to the Dragon's Eye on the kin in your neighborhood. There were *always* consequences.

So Topher got bullied by his siblings for being the youngest, by his neighborhood kin for what his mom did, and even by the Dragon's Eye themselves. Once they knew you had a snitch in the family, they made you keep snitching or they stopped protecting you from everyone else. The moment you talked to the Dragon's Eye, it became a lose-lose situation. It looked like Topher was the biggest loser of all.

Basically, he got bullied by everyone, so it was no surprise he acted like a bully too. It didn't excuse his behavior, but it did explain it. It was also no surprise that he liked the Wind Breakers. The Dragon's Eye hated them, as did the other kins, just like they all hated Topher.

Still, cheering for the Wind Breakers was dangerous, even though their pranks were usually harmless. They once filled a

City Councilor's office from floor to ceiling with dragon dung. No one was ever caught, but the Wind Breakers took credit.

Abel's downstairs neighbor's cousin once dated a boy who clicked like on a video of that poo prank, and *she* got brought in for questioning by the Dragon's Eye. She was never quite the same afterward, and she never went on a date with that boy again. No one did. He was sentenced to exile in the Farm Towers on the edge of the city just for clicking like on the wrong thing.

Topher was probably imagining the same terrible fate for himself if their teacher reported him. It was pretty cool of Instructor Ally not to. Though Topher was a jerk, he was still just barely thirteen. Thirteen-year-old jerks deserved mercy sometimes. *Sometimes.*

Abel had gotten lost in his thoughts again and hadn't heard anything that Instructor Ally explained about the pheromones and the NERDs, or how she and the Dragon Safety Officers had gotten them under control. He was annoyed with his brain for zoning out and missing such a cool story. It seemed like he was always getting distracted at the worst times. He'd have to ask Roa to tell him the story during their bus ride across town.

"I'll meet you at the bus stop," they said. "I want to talk to Instructor Ally about getting extra-credit work while we're out of school."

"Extra work?" Abel's best friend was incomprehensible to him sometimes.

They shrugged. "You should ask too. Only way to improve your grades is by actually doing schoolwork!"

"No thanks," Abel said, scuttling out of the classroom as fast as he could. "See you at the bus stop!"

• • •

"I was worried you'd bailed on me or gotten eaten or something," Abel told Roa, when they finally showed up after most of the other kids had gone.

"Nope," they said cheerfully, like they'd just come from getting ice cream, not from getting extra homework. "You know," they added, "one lucky thing about the attack closing school early is that we can go to that address your sister gave you, and still be home in time for dinner without anyone knowing where we've gone. It kinda worked out!"

"Yeah," Abel agreed. "But then also no one will know where we are if we disappear."

"Why are you worried about disappearing?" Roa was casual about the whole thing, more casual than Abel could imagine being about anything.

"Because kinners and the Dragon's Eye are after Lina over this address?" he said. "And no one else knows about it? And it's in a bad neighborhood?"

"Okay, one, we don't know that it's because of this address that they're after Lina." Roa counted off on their fingers all the reasons Abel didn't need to worry. "Two, if the Dragon's Eye is after her, then other people *do* know about it. And three, there is no such thing as a 'bad' neighborhood, just a neighborhood you don't live in. To the people who live there, it's just home."

"Yeah, home in Thunder Wings territory," Abel replied.

"The Thunder Wings aren't so bad," Roa told him.

They walked across the bridge from the platform, onto the

back of the number 17 bus, which was carried by a mint-green long-wing with piercing yellow eyes. Abel realized he was about to go the farthest from home he had ever been without an adult, and he was pretty sure he'd seen stories on the news about the area they were headed to. Maybe there was no such thing as a bad neighborhood, but there were neighborhoods where bad things happened, and this was definitely one of them. The bus took off with mighty wingbeats, and Abel's stomach lurched, though not from the dragon's flight.

"Relax," Roa tried to reassure him, yanking on their school tie to loosen it. Abel did the same. "You're about to have an adventure, like in the comics."

He looked sideways at his friend. "In Dr. Drago, innocent bystanders get devoured by dragons, like, on the regular."

Roa shrugged. "So it's better not be an innocent bystander."

"Kids are *always* innocent bystanders," Abel replied.

"Not me." Roa crossed their arms and rested their head on the glass, looking at the skyscrapers racing by outside. "I don't stand by . . . and I'm hardly innocent."

Abel laughed. It sounded like a line from a comic book, but Roa was dead serious. Abel, on the other hand, just didn't want to be dead.

As they flew through the city, Abel looked at the other passengers and wondered if they were being followed. Stop after stop, more people got off and fewer and fewer got on. The buildings got lower and lower, and less sturdy too. Some of them looked like one stray flap from the long-wing dragon might topple them.

When they reached their stop on a dismal landing tower in an empty lot, Abel heard the sound of creaking metal straining under the dragon's weight. The exit bridge hadn't even been pulled all the way back inside before the dragon pilot took off again. Clearly the pilot didn't want to stay in this part of town a moment longer than he had to.

Looking around, Abel couldn't blame him.

The landing tower was rusted and covered in graffiti, and the two buildings on either side of it were boarded and graffitied over too. There were brightly colored nicknames and messages that meant nothing to Abel, but mixed in with them was the lightning dragon of the Thunder Wings kin.

As he and Roa went down the winding metal stairs to the ground, Abel heard distant screeches and roars, the sounds of working dragons in other parts of the city. In *this* part of the city, there was quiet. Way too much quiet.

"It's creepy here," he told Roa.

His friend looked around at the boarded-up buildings and the empty streets. They didn't argue.

A light flickered over the sign for a corner store, where a bored-looking cashier sat behind a dragon-glass window, staring at his phone. He glanced up at Abel and Roa when they reached the sidewalk, then looked back down again. The sun was drooping like a tired dragon's wing, casting one side of the street into cold darkness. As Abel and Roa started walking for the address his sister had given him, they stayed on the sunny side without having to talk about it.

The warehouse had no sign nor numbers. Just a metal door set high up on a huge wall at the top of narrow metal stairs. There were landing platforms jutting out of the building above the door, but their entrances were also closed up tight with metal grates.

"You sure this is it?" Abel asked.

Roa looked at their phone and then across the street at the other warehouses, some of which did have signs and numbers. 3472: Long-Wing Limited Shipping. 3478: Golden Hoard Imports. 3482: Wyvern's Tears Medical Supply, Inc.

All the warehouses had bars on their windows and locks on their doors, but the door high in the wall above them was the only one with an electronic keycard reader.

"Yep," said Roa. "Ready?"

"Not at all," said Abel, but he led the way up the stairs. He wished his sneakers were quieter, or that the stairs weren't groaning so much. He hoped Lina wouldn't be mad at him for coming here, or for bringing a friend. She couldn't have expected him to come alone, could she? Or had she expected him not to come at all, just to keep the keycard safe?

Too late now, he thought as he slid the card from his pocket and pressed it against the panel by the door. It beeped, and there was a loud click. Roa took the handle and pulled it open.

They listened. There was no sound from inside, so Abel took a deep breath and stepped through. Roa followed him. It was dark, and they were standing on a narrow industrial catwalk, kind of like the one over the gym at school. But this one was a lot older and more rusted and missing several safety rails.

The warehouse floor was at least four stories below them. Abel couldn't make out what was down there. There were no open windows, and the only light was what streamed in through the open door behind them. He saw vague hulking shapes in the depths, and his heart leapt—dragons!—until he realized they were just pieces of factory equipment. What he'd thought were tails were conveyor belts; their great jaws were just valves and vents. It looked like the place had made cans, like the kind you'd get vegetables or beans or pangolin food in. There were lights every few feet above the catwalk, but he didn't see a switch for them.

"Hey, don't let the door clo—" he started as Roa stepped inside and it slammed shut. Darkness swallowed them, the noise of the door echoing in the warehouse. A quick push and desperate scan of the keycard told him that they were locked in. The daylight was locked on the other side.

"I don't think this is an exit," he told Roa.

"Then we've got to go through," Roa said, turning on the flashlight on their phone screen. "I mean, we were gonna have to look around anyway, right? Let's go."

Roa went forward with a confidence Abel lacked, but it was

his sister in trouble. His comic that had led them here, so he decided to fake confidence for as long as he could. Also, his phone battery wasn't charged enough to use the light and he didn't want to get left behind. He rushed right up to Roa, practically attaching himself to their back. They glanced over their shoulder at him and smiled. No one was so brave that they didn't want a friend close in an unfamiliar darkness.

Their footsteps echoed on the metal as they crept forward. Abel worried his breathing was too loud, but the place appeared abandoned. The catwalk shuddered and swayed a little with every footfall, and he couldn't wait to find the stairs, to get back onto solid ground. Even better would be to find the exit.

Roa peered over the edge as they walked, pointing their light down at tall rows of shelving, filled with unlabeled cans. They were covered in dust and cobwebs.

"Why would Lina send you to an abandoned can factory?" Roa wondered. "What would she want you to keep safe here? Mushy carrots?"

"I don't know. I think—watch out!"

He grabbed Roa's shoulder and pulled them back from an open drop where the catwalk turned and the safety railing had broken. They both fell against the side railing with a clang.

The metal screeched in protest, and the whole catwalk shook. Roa's phone fell. They gasped as it bounced off the railing, hit Abel's sneaker, and skittered to the edge, where it perched perilously.

"Stinking meatbreath!" Roa cursed as they rescued their phone and looked at the cracked screen, trying to swipe the flashlight back on. Even without the phone's light, Abel could still see Roa, and he wondered where that dim light was coming from. When he looked up, he gasped.

"Roa! Look!"

The stars were out. An amazing, crystal clear field of stars twinkled above them and in front of them where the railing had broken. Abel had never seen stars so crisp before; there were constellations he didn't recognize, galaxies and nebulae and thousands of perfect, blazing points of light.

On most nights, it was hard to see any stars at all because the lights of buildings and billboards and business signs and lane markers were too bright. It took Abel's breath away.

"How can we see so many stars?" he asked, because Roa knew things about science.

"How can we see stars at all?" Roa replied.

"There must be a hole in the roof," Abel suggested. "Maybe that's why the place was abandoned. The buildings here aren't very well made."

"No," Roa said. "I mean, how can we see stars when it's still daylight outside?"

Abel frowned. When they'd gone inside, the sun was nowhere near setting. As he looked closer, the stars in front of him wavered and bent, like they were lights hanging on a giant black sheet hung across the warehouse.

In the center of that deep black sheet, two bright orange eyes slitted open.

"This isn't the sky," Roa whispered, then screamed. "A Sunrise Reaper!"

"A what?" Abel asked. But just below the opening orange

eyes, he got his answer. A ball of orange fire formed in the black, growing like a sunrise, until it was bright enough for Abel to see it was forming at the back of a huge dragon's throat.

The Sunrise Reaper was perched on a high loading dock across from them, its wide black wings spread to show glistening lights that covered its entire underside. When hunting at night, it must have camouflaged with the sky itself. Then, when it fired its breath weapons, its victims would be mesmerized by the sudden sunrise. They'd only realize they were being hunted the instant before the dragon's breath incinerated them.

For Abel and Roa, this was that instant.

"Jump!" Abel yelled as the fireball erupted from the dragon's mouth.

Abel threw himself over the side of the railing, grabbing on to edge of the catwalk and dangling over the factory floor. Roa dangled opposite him as a streak of hot orange flame burst against the very spot where they'd been standing. The metal warmed against Abel's palms, the catwalk heating like a pan on a stove.

The fire breath stopped, and soon only the stars on the dragon's scales lit the dim warehouse. He and Roa still hung off opposite sides of the catwalk, four stories in the air.

Abel's arms burned from the strain, and his hands felt like they were being cooked on a waffle iron. But he couldn't let go, or he'd be splattered to paste on the concrete floor below.

There was a great creaking of metal as the huge dragon shifted its weight. The false stars on its body shifted nauseatingly. It bent its neck to peer at Abel. Its huge black snout nearly touched him as its orange eyes widened; its face was bigger than his whole body. The dragon pressed its nose against Abel and sniffed.

"Ugh," he groaned. "It smells like grilled garbage."

The dragon opened its mouth, and Abel saw the start of another sunrise forming in front of him. This time, there would be no escape. *He* was the garbage that was about to get grilled.

"Sorry! Sorry! I didn't mean that!"

He could see its fangs in the silhouette of its growing flame. Even the smallest of its teeth was bigger than his forearm. He thought about letting himself fall, wondering which would hurt less, breaking every bone in his body or being cooked alive. Both ended with him getting eaten. Then he remembered the video Silas had shown them of Lina breaking into a rich person's stables to steal a dragon . . . probably *this* dragon. "Lina sent me!" he yelled. "I'm here to help!"

The dragon paused. Abel had no idea if it could understand him. Different dragons had different levels of intelligence, but it's not like they spoke human languages. They spoke in clicks and grunts and screeches and growls. But maybe it could tell by his tone that he wasn't a threat. Or maybe he just didn't smell delicious anymore. Either way, the flame in its throat died down.

"I'm gonna pull myself up now, okay?" he said to the dragon, trying to keep his tone light and friendly. "Please don't cook me? Just, like . . . be cool? Can you be cool? You look cool. I mean, like, the whole night-sky thing? That's cool."

He began to do his best pull-up, which was not very good at all.

"ERRRRRR . . ." He strained, flexing every muscle he had.

His elbows, however, barely bent. He kicked his legs furiously, like he was air swimming. It was no use. He couldn't do it; he couldn't lift himself.

Suddenly, the dragon put its hard snout below his feet and nodded, tossing him into the air and letting him land with a clang on his side on the catwalk. Roa pulled themself up on their own, just after Abel. The dragon looked down at both of them, with its head cocked to the side.

"Look, he's hurt!" Roa said, pointing to a shimmering silver spot on the dragon's wing. It looked like a couple of the stars leaking into one another. "Sunrise Reapers have glowing silver blood; that's how they create the illusion of starlight. It looks like that part of his wing is bleeding."

The dragon turned its head and looked at its wound, then back at them.

"How do you know it's a him?" Abel asked. "He's not wearing his pronouns on a name tag."

"Male Sunrise Reapers have orange eyes," Roa said. "Females have red or yellow."

"But what if he's nonbinary?" Abel wondered. "And we've offended him."

"Then he'll eat us." Roa considered it. "I can respect that."

Abel balked as his best friend laughed.

The orange-eyed dragon loomed over them, looking quizzically between him and Roa, like he was still considering if they were food or friends.

"Anyway," Roa said. "I've studied these kinds of wounds in my after-school classes. I think I can fix it if—"

Roa stepped forward, and the dragon lunged, snapping its

jaws. Roa jumped back just in time, but Abel leapt forward and rested his hand on the side of the dragon's face.

"It's okay; they're a friend," he said before he even realized what he'd just done. Who leaps to put their hand on an angry dragon's face? And why was he so sure the dragon would listen to him or even want to be touched by him?

But he did.

The Sunrise Reaper stopped his attack and looked at him with one orange eye. He didn't dare move. His hand rested on black scales that were warm as bathwater but hard as metal.

"It's okay," he repeated, both to the dragon and to Roa. "It's all okay."

Roa took a deep breath and stepped forward. The dragon shifted his weight and lowered his wing so they had access to the wound. Roa began to inspect the injury by the light of the creature's own blood, which was too weird for Abel to get his head around. He'd have liked to see more than the gleaming false stars and the wary orange eye, but now that he was stuck standing still like this, he had time to wonder again why his sister would have stashed an injured dragon—an injured *stolen* dragon—in a can factory on the far side of town.

"I'm going to need some medical putty," Roa said. "And sterile wire to stitch the wound closed."

"Um . . . okay, where are we supposed to get that?" he asked.

"Don't be mad," Roa said.

"Huh?" Abel was confused again, a feeling he was fast getting used to. "Mad about what?"

"I asked for help."

"But your phone's busted?"

"I asked . . . um . . . before . . . when we were still at school." Roa sounded apologetic. "When you told me the story. I kind of figured what Lina might have hidden here and I knew we'd need help."

"At *school*? Who did you ask at school?"

"*Whom,*" Roa corrected him.

"Don't. Do. That. Now." Abel didn't like that Roa had told people about this when they'd sworn not to; they'd sworn on a secret! "Who?" he demanded. "Who did you tell?"

"Us," a new voice barked from the darkness, just before the factory lights snapped on. They were no longer alone. Instead, they were surrounded by kinners.

"The Thunder Wings," Roa said. "My kin."

10

"YOU'RE IN A *KIN*?" ABEL'S stomach dropped,
along with his jaw.

"Well," Roa said, "I'm more like an apprentice."

"To the Thunder Wings?" Abel closed his jaw but could do
nothing about his sinking stomach. The betrayal stung. First
Lina, and now Roa.

Did *everyone* have some secret criminal life he didn't know
about? Roa themself had said it: Secrets were like dragon's bile,
they stunk up friendships. (Okay, he couldn't remember exactly
what they'd said.) The point was that they were keeping a huge
secret to themself, even as they told Abel not to!

"I'm not, like, a full kinner," Roa clarified. "I don't rob anyone. I don't have tattoos."

"Yeah, but they sure do!" Abel looked around at the Thunder
Wings who surrounded them.

There were a dozen fierce kinners in the warehouse, six on
the catwalks on either side of the huge dragon, and another six
on the ground four stories below.

The ones on the catwalk had large stun sticks, like the Dragon
Safety Officers at school. They pointed these at the Sunrise
Reaper. The spears gave a shock specifically designed to get
through a full-sized dragon's scales. They were illegal for anyone
without a license, because a shock that could stun a dragon

could kill a human in a half a heartbeat. These kinners didn't look like they'd applied for licenses at city hall.

The Thunder Wings had a kind of uniform. They wore clothes that were mixes of grays and whites and pale blues and purples. Over their clothes they all wore heavy smocks, like veterinarians, but covered with sewed-in pockets where they kept weapons and tools. All their smocks were embroidered with the Thunder Wings symbol, the lightning dragon. And all the kinners had the same symbol tattooed on them somewhere too.

And that's when Abel realized how Roa had gotten them a message about the warehouse.

Instructor Ally had the Thunder Wings tattoo. She wasn't a former kinner. She was *still* a kinner! Roa hadn't gone back for extra homework at all!

"You told our *teacher*?" he groaned.

Seventh grade was generally as lawless and wild as any kin war, but it did have its own set of rules. One of them was that you didn't tell the teacher *anything* if you could avoid it, even a teacher as cool as Instructor Ally.

"She's in my kin," Roa said quietly. "I hope you understand. I *had* to."

The Sunrise Reaper grunted. His eyes darted over the newly arrived kinners, but he didn't move. Abel still had his hand on the dragon's snout. His four thin fingers were the only thing keeping the fire breather calm. He used his thumb to stroke the dragon's scales, the same way he did to make Percy coo. Of course, this dragon could've swallowed his pet pangolin without chewing if it wanted to.

All his life, Abel had admired and feared dragons; he thought he'd never get close to a cool one, but now his little hand was taming one of the coolest ones he'd ever seen. His pulse thumped from his chest to his fingers. His cheeks flushed. He felt . . . powerful.

He wished he didn't also feel betrayed at the same time.

"You should've told me," he said to Roa.

"I couldn't," Roa said. "For your own safet—"

"Don't," he interrupted them. "I don't want to hear anyone tell me something is for my own safety ever again. What you really mean is, it was easier."

"My parents couldn't afford my after-school dragon care classes." Roa sounded a little desperate. "But the kin offered to pay . . . in exchange for work. When they need little dragon care jobs done, I do them. I sew stitches and administer medicine. It's a great way to learn, and to pay back what my parents owe. Instructor Ally keeps an eye on me, to make sure I don't get into anything *too* dangerous. I never meant to lie to you. I just couldn't tell you."

The Thunder Wings were the knowledge-loving kin, so it made sense that they'd have infiltrated a school, but it bothered Abel that they'd use Roa like that . . . and that Roa would let them. Roa loved school and wanted to do well; if their teacher worked for the kin, then the kin could decide what Roa's grades would be. If Roa got out of line, they could make sure those grades suffered. The kins used people the way they used dragons. They took what they wanted from whoever had it, whether it was money or knowledge or work, and they made it impossible to say no. Maybe Abel could forgive them. He could at least try.

"You did well, Roa," one of the kinners said. He didn't seem even slightly afraid of the huge black dragon looming nearby.

"Thank you, Olus," Roa replied.

Olus walked right past Abel and the dragon's nose, handing a medical bag to Roa so they could start stitching the wounded wing. Then he turned back around to meet the dragon's eyes.

"So this is the dreaded Karak," Olus said. The dragon snorted at what must have been his name.

Nice to meet you, Karak, Abel thought. *Please don't eat me.*

Olus turned to Abel. "Your sister is very gifted, to steal a dragon with this pedigree. Perhaps it runs in the family?" He looked Abel up and down, lingering on the hand Abel still had on the side of the dragon's face. "Perhaps not. I suppose we'll know soon enough."

"How do you know my sister?" Abel asked.

Olus smiled. He had huge blond mutton chops and wild hair that shot out in all directions, like someone being electrocuted. He looked about as old as Abel's dad, but much more thickly built, with pocked cheeks and heavy eyebrows that shaded small, dark, and searching eyes. His hands were like two slabs of meat, and he wore long fingerless gloves over them. The shirt below his smock had no sleeves. Abel followed the colorful tattoos up and down his massive arms. They told a story Abel couldn't quite understand, but from the few images he *could* make out, the story was crude and violent and more than a little upsetting. How could his best friend work for a man like this?

"Lina has gotten too bold," Olus explained. While Roa worked on the dragon, Abel kept his hand exactly where it was. If he moved it, Karak might bite Roa's head off. He was still mad, but his unmoving hand was the start of forgiveness. You couldn't forgive your best friend once you let them get eaten.

"This dragon belonged to a very powerful person," Olus said. "Its egg had been smuggled into the city at great cost, and it was being raised with the best care for the Red Talons kin." Olus laughed at some passing thought he didn't choose to share. "Your sister's kin, the Sky Knights, decided to relieve its owner of the dragon to use it in the next battle for themselves. Sadly, it was injured in the escape. The Red Talons chased her, and your sister decided to hide it here, in *our* territory. Of course, she didn't expect us to find it in one warehouse out of hundreds, but thanks to you, we have. Now Karak will fight for *us*."

"You're going to steal this dragon to battle it?" Abel shook his head. "But you just said he's not yours."

This time, everyone laughed. "Finders keepers is the law of Drakopolis, boy," Olus said. "It's the only law that really matters in this city. Whoever controls the most dragons has the most power. And with your help, that *will* be us."

"*My* help?" Abel shook his head. He thought about the Red Talons' threats against his family. Whatever the Thunder Wings said, his family still lived in Red Talons territory. Plus, the Dragon's Eye was still after Lina—and *they* controlled more dragons than all the kins combined. Aiding the Thunder Wings would just put his own family in even more danger.

And besides, he wasn't sure how he *could* help them anyway.

"Take your hand off Karak," Olus said.

"Um . . ." Abel hesitated.

"Now!" Olus commanded so loudly that even the dragon flinched.

Abel took his hand away, and almost instantly, Karak reared back, rising to his full height. The dragon's head nearly vanished into the darkness high above. He spread his wide wings, showing the place where Roa had just barely finished stitching. Karak looked down and roared.

The building shook. In the light, Abel could see that Karak's scales were a mix of different shades of black, not one solid color. He could see the veins and sacks in his wings that created the starlight illusion, and his blinking fury. Being a nocturnal dragon, he was confused and nervous in the light. Abel might not be a genius like Roa, but he knew that a confused and nervous dragon was a dangerous dragon. The growing ring of fire in his mouth confirmed that.

"Call it off," Olus said to Abel.

"What? Me?" Abel asked.

"Call it off or we'll have to use the stun sticks," Olus said.

"No, don't!" Roa pleaded.

"It's not up to me." Olus shrugged.

Abel looked up at the dragon, preparing his blast of sun-hot flame.

"Stop?" he said, way too quietly for the dragon to hear. "Um . . . Karak? Hey! You! Um . . . Calm down?"

"Are you asking it or telling it?" Olus barked.

"Oh . . . okay, right . . ." Abel cleared his throat. "Karak! It's okay! Come back down! Right . . . er . . . NOW!"

The dragon cocked his head again, uncertain, but slowed his wingbeats. The fire simmering in his throat faded, and then he lowered himself back to the catwalk, which squealed under his weight. Olus grinned.

"And there it is," he said. "It seems the dragon's bonded to you. Which means we have our rider for the battle."

"What? Me? *What?*" A charge ran through Abel's body like he'd just been struck with a stun stick himself. It was one thing to calm a dragon down out of desperation, another thing entirely to become a dragon rider for a kin battle. He couldn't even tame a NERD!

"It likes you," Olus said. "Perhaps your sister did such a good job bonding to it, it senses that you're family. Dragons are loners by nature. Family bonds are mysterious to them. We don't really know how or what they perceive, especially breeds as rare as this one. It doesn't matter for our purposes, as long as it feels a kinship with you. You'll have to fly it for us."

"But I . . ." Abel wasn't even sure where to start listing the reasons he couldn't fly a Sunrise Reaper in an illegal dragon battle for the Thunder Wings kin.

"You will begin training tomorrow," Olus said. "Convenient that your school is closed, no? Thank your sister for us."

"I—what? Lina?"

Olus laughed. "The Wind Breakers would never attack a school like that," he said. "A Sky Knights operative stole a sizable amount of gaseous pheromone from one of our labs last night, just after your sister vanished. It seems *they* wanted your school shut down too. They just didn't know we'd find you here first."

"But . . ." Abel didn't know what to say. Had Lina's kin really arranged to close his school so that he'd go look after her stolen dragon? His fists clenched. He was already tired of being used and lied to. The moment he saw Lina again, he planned to have some very strong words with her, words he probably wasn't supposed to know.

"Your instructor will meet you here every day," Olus continued. "As long as you win this battle for us, you will be perfectly safe. We can even help your family out with some of its financial troubles." Olus patted him on the shoulder, a gesture with much more malice than affection in it. "Just remember, this isn't school. There are no grades. Failure here will *not* go well for you, nor for anyone you care about." The kin leader took a deep breath and looked around. "Okay then. We'll leave you to feed your dragon and get yourselves home."

"But what about the Red Talons?" Abel asked.

Olus shrugged. "Not really my problem, is it?" He whistled, and his kinners broke their formation, melting into the rows of dusty cans and broken machinery.

"Wings wide, my young friend! Wings wide!" Olus cheered. "Like or not, you're a dragon rider now! Congratulations."

With that, he left Abel and Roa alone with Karak looking down at them in the dark once more.

"I am so, so, so, so sorry that you got caught up in this," Roa said.

"What was that word we learned in vocabulary last week?" Abel asked. "It means when you're so shocked and angry that you, like, can't even?"

"Nonplussed?" Roa suggested.

"Yeah, that," Abel said. "I am so, so, *so nonplussed* that I can't even."

"I'm really sorry that I—" Roa tried again, but was interrupted by the sound of mooing.

They leaned over the railing and looked down at the factory floor. There the Thunder Wings had left a large cow behind, softly munching a pile of grass in the dim light. It seemed unaware of the two children and the dark black dragon above.

"Oh no," Abel groaned. "Is a Sunrise Reaper a—"

"Charivore," Roa sighed. Karak turned his head toward the cow. His mouth became a ring of fire, growing like a summer sunrise.

Abel shut his eyes as his new partner cooked dinner.

When he opened his eyes again, there was nothing but a charred spot on the floor where the cow had been. Karak settled down on top of a big tin rolling machine to take a nap. His massive snores rattled the rusted machine.

"How am I supposed to fly a battle dragon?" Abel wondered, stomach churning.

"Same way you learned to play DrakoTek," Roa answered. "Practice."

Abel didn't mention how he'd played DrakoTek for years and hadn't gotten any good at it. Also, DrakoTek cards wouldn't get you and your family eaten by a dragon, killed by a kin, or sent to prison if you lost. Battling real dragons in a street fight was nothing like a card game.

"Nonplussed," Abel repeated the word. "I am definitely *nonplussed*."

PART TWO

"NICE TO MEET YOU; PLEASE
DON'T EAT ME."

11

TRAINING STARTED BEFORE SUNRISE THE next morning.

Abel had planned to tell his parents an elaborate story about needing to help Roa with an early morning science project for the entire time that school was closed, but before he even got home from the can factory that night, Instructor Ally had already shown up at his apartment.

"Ah, Abel, thank you for helping with the *cleanup* after school today," his treacherous teacher said the moment he walked in the door. She was sitting in the living room with his parents, sipping firegrass tea. She had crumbs from one of his favorite Wing Scout Cookies lingering on her scarf, and he just *knew* it'd been the last one in the box.

Ally winked at him, a signal to play it cool. Abel was covered in soot and sweat and maybe a little charred cow meat, so he probably *did* look like he'd been scouring floors in the aftermath of a dragon attack. "I was just telling your parents what a help you were after the disaster today. And we had the idea that, since school is closed, maybe you can *keep* helping me for the rest of the term."

"Helping you?" Abel asked numbly. He was still thinking about the ten-ton dragon the color of the night sky that he'd left in a can warehouse on the other side of town. And also about how much he'd wanted that Wing Scout Cookie for himself. It was chocolate graham cracker and caramel, the best one. He didn't think adults even *liked* that sort of thing, let alone teachers who were secretly kinners.

Maybe she'd just eaten it to show him she could? Somehow, sitting on the couch with his parents, devouring his favorite cookie, was more intimidating than all the threats the other kinners had made. Instructor Ally was too cool to break anything, but she didn't need to. Real power didn't have to flex its muscles.

"Instructor Ally thinks it would be good to prevent any backsliding while school is closed," his mom chimed in eagerly. "Your grades haven't been the best, and with everything going on . . ." Her voice trailed off. His mom wasn't about to tell his teacher that dangerous Red Talons kinners were after his big sister. She didn't know that his teacher already knew all about it.

Abel noticed that Ally was wearing a jacket to cover her tattoos. He also noticed it was gray and pale blue and purple, the Thunder Wings colors. Subtle. He had to remember that. His teacher was *very* subtle.

"We think it'd be good for you," his dad added, then coughed a little. "Give some structure to your days. No sense sitting around the house with me all the time."

"Wonderful!" Instructor Ally nodded. She slapped her palms on her knees and stood, then thanked his parents for the tea and the cookies, and turned to Abel. "Get some rest tonight, Abel. We start tomorrow at sunrise."

She winked at him on the word "sunrise."

On her way out, Instructor Ally glanced both ways down the hall. She was probably nervous to be a Thunder Wings operative in Red Talons territory. Then she flipped her collar up and tossed the thick coils of hair back over her shoulder, and walked to the elevators like she didn't have a care in the world.

Maybe because all her cares had been laid squarely on Abel's narrow shoulders.

His parents looked so relieved, believing that Abel would be safe with his teacher—occupied while they dealt with the trouble Lina had gotten into. They had no idea that he was neck-deep in Lina's troubles. How had it not even been twenty-four hours since cleaning night? And where under flaming skies had Lina run off to?

"Why don't you take a shower before dinner?" his father suggested. "You smell like a NERD's feeding trough."

"And for after dinner, I got a treat," his mom added, opening a kitchen cabinet and showing him a brand-new, unopened box of Wing Scout Cookies. Abel could've cried. Sometimes a box of cookies was so much more than a box of cookies.

He wanted to hug his mom and bury his face in her sweater and tell his parents everything that had happened. He didn't know what to do and just wanted his mom and dad to make it all better . . .

But no. That was for little kids. He was a dragon rider now, bound to a rare and valuable dragon. He was going to have to figure this problem out on his own. Like Dr. Drago said in the Holiday Special Issue: *A hero does what is needed, even when it's hard. But not if it's evil. Then, you know . . . he doesn't.*

Now that Abel thought about it, the writing in that comic wasn't always very good. He probably needed something better to base his entire life philosophy on.

• • •

There was no life philosophy that made it easier to wake up at the crack of dawn and take the number 5 bus to the number 17 bus to the old can factory all on his own, but that was Abel's morning.

Bleary-eyed, with nothing but a cold breakfast bar and glass of Sunberry juice in his stomach, he arrived at the top of the tall metal stairs and let himself in with Lina's keycard. The warehouse lights were already on. Roa and Instructor Ally were there, and Karak was curled up on top of a huge pile of cans and fallen shelves, and a safe that looked like it had been ripped out of a wall. (There were pieces of drywall still attached.) The dragon was sound asleep, still snoring.

"He made himself a hoard," Roa told Abel, instead of saying *Hello* or *Good morning* or *Sorry I betrayed you and your family to a kin you didn't even know I was a part of.* "Dragons will gather whatever is shiniest or most valuable to people and assemble it into their hoard."

"Yeah," Abel grumbled at them. "I know."

"I'm just telling you because that's kind of important for how kin battles work," Roa replied. There was still tension between them, but Roa was obviously done trying to apologize. Maybe Abel just needed to move on too.

"I know how kin battles work," Abel snapped. He hadn't moved on yet. Roa frowned, but it was Ally who answered.

"You only *think* you know," she said. "But what you've read in comics and seen in movies is nothing compared to the reality . . . which is why we're going to let the dragon sleep a bit longer while you answer some questions."

"You're giving me a *quiz*?" Abel shook his head and looked to Roa with dismay. He'd never imagined becoming an illegal battle dragon rider would be just like school.

Making it even more like school, Topher appeared from behind one of the machines, mop in hand, a sour expression on his face.

"What is *he* doing here?" Abel asked.

"I asked the same thing," Roa added.

"He's my intern," Ally explained. "His family, like your own, thought it best if he worked for the duration of the school term. You can ignore him. He'll only speak when spoken to."

"I finished cleaning the bathrooms," Topher whined. "Can I please have a break now?"

"He will only speak when spoken to!" Ally repeated without looking at him. "Otherwise, he will stand quietly and await instructions. Or we can pay his parents another visit?"

Topher's shoulders slumped, and Ally returned her attention to Abel. "What is the goal of a dragon battle?" she asked.

"To capture the hoard," Abel answered, glad for an easy question.

"Correct," said Ally. "And what is the hoard?"

Abel looked over at Karak. The black dragon was snoozing atop his pile of improvised, and mostly worthless, treasure.

"Whatever is shiniest or seems most valuable." Abel quoted what Roa had just said to him. He gave his friend an apprecia-tive nod.

"But what does that mean in a dragon battle?" Ally pressed him.

"It's . . . uh . . . whatever they want it to be?" Abel didn't quite know. In the movies and comics, it was always different stuff, like a flag with the kin's symbol on it, or a valuable piece of art. Or even an actual treasure.

Ally shook her head and spoke in her teacher voice. "The hoard in a dragon battle is a symbolic token of the kin that has issued the challenge. It is given value by its importance to the kin. Whoever captures the symbolic hoard and gets it back to their lair first wins the battle. Tell me: What is the lair?"

"It's where a dragon lives," Abel said.

"In a dragon battle, the lair is also symbolic," Ally corrected him. "It's a circle on the ground at the start of the match."

"Why not just call them circles, then?" Abel wondered. "Is everything in a kin battle symbolic?"

"Not everything. The violence, I assure you, is quite real," Ally said. "Once the dragons launch from their *lairs*, the match is a very real game of offense and defense with life-or-death stakes."

Abel looked over at the sleeping dragon. Three parallel lines of small black horns began behind his eyes and went all the way back to where the wings met the body. The way Karak had curled up, Abel could only see one of his massive feet hanging out along the pile of expired lima beans. But that one foot was bigger than Abel's whole body. The claws on the ends of Karak's toes looked like they could open a can the size of a building. Abel couldn't imagine how there'd be a dragon more ferocious in a kin battle, and the thought made his chest puff a little with pride. *That dragon chose me*, he thought. *And I'm gonna be great.*

Then he remembered what his sister told him, about the great dragon riders being the ones you never heard about, because they never got caught. His teacher had gotten caught and sent to Windlee Prison for it. Did he really think he could be better than *her*?

"Wings wide," Roa reassured him. "You can do this."

He smiled. They were still on his side and he was glad for it. Maybe he *had* moved on from their betrayal. It felt good to let go of a grudge.

"The kin battles are equal parts race, heist, and duel," Ally explained. "You will work with your dragon to master all three aspects, or you're certain to fail."

"So . . . which did *you* fail?" Topher asked. Roa gasped, and Ally looked like she was about to eat the boy. Abel wondered why Topher seemed incapable of just shutting his mouth. Wasn't he in enough trouble? Abel bulged his eyes to signal that Topher should just keep quiet, but Topher barreled on. "What? We're not supposed to know? I mean, what went wrong? How'd you end up in Windlee?"

Ally took a deep breath and exhaled slowly. Topher gripped his mop harder, bracing himself for something, but the teacher still refused to look at him. "This is actually good for Abel to know," she said. "I got caught because I forgot the most important thing about any kin battle: No one wins alone. I had a ground crew, as you will have, but I also had a few big victories and let them go to my head. My ground crew got tired of my attitude, and when the Dragon's Eye showed up to make arrests, my crew disappeared into the night. Leaving me surrounded. I could've fought my way out, maybe, but it's hard to fight when your heart is broken. I knew my friends had left me, and knew I deserved it. I surrendered, took the fall, and did my time. But I stayed loyal to my crew, and to my kin, even when the Dragon's Eye questioned me without mercy. The kin rewarded me for my loyalty. They let me back in, helped me get a job in the school, and now they're giving me this chance. You, Abel, will be my redemption too. Your success is my success, you understand? We're in this together."

Ally smiled, and there was even kindness in her eyes. She seemed like his teacher again. He felt safe.

But then she added, "So, if you're gonna be dragon food, best get it over with early. Time to wake you partner for the first lesson."

Without further ado, Ally grabbed a loose wrench that was lying on the floor near her feet and threw it at the sleeping dragon. It bounced harmlessly off Karak's scales and clattered onto the dragon's hoarded cans, knocking a few loose. They rolled away across the factory floor.

The dragon snapped one eye open and locked it on Abel. Topher leapt behind his mop, like the handle could hide him.

One thing even Topher knew, bad a student as he was, was never to disturb a sleeping dragon.

12

CLATTER, CLANK, CLINK.

The loose cans rolled to a stop, then silence fell. The sounds of the city vanished. The sounds of Ally's, Topher's, and Roa's breathing vanished. The only thing Abel could hear was the thud-thump of his heartbeat as Karak raised his massive head and glowered at him.

Is that the word? he wondered. *Glowered?* It didn't sound hungry enough. There had to be a word that sounded more like threatening to eat someone with a look.

He was doing the thing again, letting his mind wander when he was stressed. He stopped thinking about vocab and looked back up at the glowering dragon.

"Um . . . hey, pal," he offered with a meek wave. "Sleep well?"

"RAWREEEE!" Karak replied, a screeching roar that curled Abel's toes and knocked him flat on his bottom. The dragon leapt from the pile of cans and landed with his giant forepaws on either side of Abel. His head pressed Abel down to the floor with hot breath. Just inches from Abel's face, he sniffed, scalding and wet.

That did wonders for Abel's focus. He was not distracted now. He was, on the other hand, terrified.

"Uh, sorry to wake you," Abel offered, wiping the dragon snot off his face. He pushed himself up onto his elbows. "I just . . . want to, uh . . . I wasn't . . . er, stealing your cans? They're right there?" He pointed at the cans that had rolled away and wished everything he said wasn't coming out like a question.

The dragon swung his head toward his hoard, then toward Abel, blasting him with another puff of hot nostril steam. The force of it blew Abel's hair around. The dragon then sat back on his haunches and waited. He hadn't eaten Abel yet, so that was good. But now what?

"Karak is a Sunrise Reaper," Ally said. She was leaning on one of the tin rolling machines. Roa was standing slightly behind her, trying to look just as calm, but failing. "What do you know about Sunrise Reapers?"

"A Reaper is a medium-sized dragon of the medium-wing class," Roa answered. "The Sunrise Reaper is a nocturnal charivore, meaning it hunts at night and must cook its meat before eating it."

"Thank you, Roa," Ally said. "But I was asking Abel."

"Uh, what Roa said," Abel told her.

"Stop saying 'uh,'" Ally snapped at him. "A rider must present confidence, even if they do not feel confident, lest they make their dragon skittish and uncertain. Do you want a skittish and uncertain dragon?"

"Uh . . . no," Abel said uncertainly.

"Then stand up straight and greet your partner properly. Reapers are proud creatures and will not be piloted by the timid or the disrespectful."

"Okay," Abel said, taking a hesitant step toward the dragon. *His* dragon, he thought.

"Wait!" Roa stepped over to him. They dropped wireless ear-buds into his hand. "So we can communicate."

"Where did you *get* these?" he wondered. The earbuds were state-of-the-art; there was no way Roa could afford them. There was no way anyone in their whole lousy *school* could afford them. Except . . .

Then he remembered: except the ones in a kin. Like Roa. Like Abel himself now too.

They smiled. "The kin takes care of its own. So, get to it, dragon rider."

Roa gave him a gentle shoulder squeeze and then retreated to the safety of the large machine.

Abel put the earbuds in, and Ally's voice came through, as clear as if she was standing next to him. "Introduce yourself properly," she said.

"HELLO, KARAK," he said loudly. Then, thinking about a dragon's pride, he bowed from the waist. "It is an honor to see you again! I'm sorry for the way we met last night! I didn't mean to startle you!" He figured the dragon owed him an apology for nearly incinerating him, but he wasn't going to hold his breath. Dragons didn't apologize. "My name's Abel! You know my sister!"

The dragon seemed to relax. His head lowered and rose once, which Abel figured was a nod.

"Loudness isn't the same as confidence," Ally coached him. "It's often the opposite. Now, ask permission to climb onto his back."

"Just like that?" Abel whispered, overcompensating for his previous shouts. "I don't need, like, lessons before I get on?"

"Getting on *is* your lesson," Ally said.

"Right . . ." Abel took another step forward. "May I, uh, climb aboard you, please?"

"That will never work," Ally said. "You have to sound sure of yourself."

"WW3D," Roa added.

Abel stuck out his chest. "WW3D," he replied. He put one foot in front of the other, filling himself with borrowed bravery.

"Karak," he declared. "I want to climb onto your back. May I?"

Again, the dragon bobbed his head. Abel glanced back once at Roa, who gave him a thumbs-up. Then he took another step forward, and another, looking for a way on. In the movies, it looked so easy.

"*WW3D,*" he whispered to himself, forgetting they could hear him through the earbuds. "*WW3D, WW3D, WW3D.*"

"What is that? A code?" Ally asked.

"Nothing," he and Roa said at the same time.

"*Everything* means *something*," Ally grunted, but didn't press them.

The dragon snorted and shifted his weight from foot to foot. Karak's patience would not last forever.

The bus driver boards a dragon every day, Abel thought. *If he can do it, you can do it.*

Of course, a long-wing dragon with a bus attached and no power in its breath was as much like a Sunrise Reaper as . . . well, Abel couldn't think of anything to compare it to. They were both dragons, which was about where their similarities ended. A Sunrise Reaper was a weapon; a bus-hauling long-wing was just a bus.

Abel walked to the side of Karak's great body, standing halfway between the head and shoulder. The dragon lowered his chin toward the floor so that his neck was stretched out and the top was just a little above Abel. He reached up and grabbed one of the thick spines that ran from the base of his skull to the tip of his tail. It was smooth and strangely warm. Almost hot. Abel used it to hoist himself up, while trying to throw his leg over Karak's thick neck at the same time.

All he succeeded in doing was slipping off sideways and landing on the floor.

Karak turned back to look at him. The dragon narrowed his great orange eyes.

"I got this; don't worry," Abel said, brushing himself off and reaching up to grab the knob of spine again. This time he jumped as he pulled himself up and threw his leg over, but instead of letting him fall, Karak bent his neck with Abel's jump. The dragon tossed him into the air and onto his back with a hard thump, right between the spurs of his spine. Had Abel landed a hand's width forward or backward, he'd have gotten dragon-spiked right between his legs. Instead, he settled onto the huge neck with surprising comfort, legs dangling on either side.

"What now?" he asked. But before Roa or Ally could answer, Karak raised his head, bent his legs, and launched himself into the air.

Abel's neck jolted back, and he was pressed down against the dragon's scales. He wrapped his arms around Karak's neck and squeezed his legs, holding on for dear life as the floor fell away.

Suddenly, Karak's wings snapped open. He stopped in midair, nearly knocking Abel off.

"AH!" Abel yelled.

Karak hovered halfway between the floor and the ceiling. Abel squeezed the knot of bone on Karak's back so hard he thought his knuckles might bust through his skin.

"Don't riders usually have saddles and harnesses?" he called, adjusting his grip so he was basically lying down against the dragon's neck, arms wrapped around it in a hug.

"You have to *earn* your saddle first," Ally replied.

"If you tried to harness Karak the first time you rode him, he'd definitely eat you," Roa explained. "Even the tamest dragon has to give permission to be harnessed. Building trust is the key to everything that comes next."

"Okay . . . so how do I do that?" Abel asked. The dragon shifted against his own wingbeats, rocking in the air. Abel tried to keep steady. His legs felt weak and tingly. The floor looked *really* far below.

"Tell him where to go," Ally said.

"Use your—" Roa started, but Ally cut them off.

"You must have an instinct for this," she said. "Your ground crew can't tell you how to fly."

"But you're not my ground crew!" Abel said with some desperation. "You're my teacher."

"Sorry, you broke up there," Ally replied, crystal clear. He knew she was lying, but also that he'd get no help by pleading. "I urge you to do *something*. A Sunrise Reaper isn't going to wait all day, and when he *tires* of waiting, he might decide you're a better meal than you are a rider."

Abel thought a prayer so loud he was worried his earbuds could pick it up. He squeezed the dragon's neck with his knees, leaning his whole weight to the left.

Like a single leaf bending the branch of a mighty tree, the huge dragon turned.

Abel nearly slipped off again and had to quickly right himself. As soon as he did, the dragon leveled off. He leaned the other way, and Karak obeyed.

"Okay, you're turning in place," Roa said. "Maybe try going forward, toward that huge door over there."

Abel looked along the length of Karak's neck and saw giant doors to the next part of the warehouse. It was bathed in dim auxiliary lighting and so large that three dragons could fly the whole length of it side by side, with room to spare for turning. Was this why Lina had hidden Karak here? Did she know he'd need space to train?

"How do I—" he started, but stopped himself before Ally could scold him again. He'd have to figure it out on his own.

He tried leaning back. Karak rose so high Abel nearly got squashed against the ceiling. He leaned forward, and Karak lowered himself, settling down to just above the floor. His wings beat steadily to hold them in place, the wind knocking empty cans this way and that.

"Hey, Karak!" Abel called up the neck. The dragon bent his head clear around, to look down his own spine at Abel. "So . . . uh . . . what do you think about flying forward?"

Later, Abel wouldn't be sure about what he saw, but in that

moment, he could've sworn the dragon smirked. Karak turned his head straight, stretched his spine, and launched forward through the door with a stomach-flattening WHOOOOOSH!

"AHHHHH!" Abel screamed as the dragon charged through the air, blurring the emergency lights as they zoomed past and zipping straight for the far side of the factory. They were headed for a wall of boarded-up windows.

"Okay, pal, slow down! Watch out for the windows!" Abel called, but Karak showed no signs of slowing.

"He's making a break for it," Roa warned over the earbuds.

"Steer, Abel!" Ally barked.

"He's gonna be meat paste!" Topher exclaimed so loudly that Roa's earbuds picked up the sound.

"Karak!" Abel yelled. He leaned back and to the side as hard as he could. "Turn!"

Just before the pair burst through the wood and glass that would've surely shredded Abel into boy-sized ribbons, Karak swooped up and turned in the direction Abel was leaning. The claws at the end of his right wing cut deep grooves in the wooden window frames, grooves that burned black as the claws pulled away. But they held in place.

Now they were facing the other way, heading straight back for the machine shop where they'd started.

Abel leaned forward, lowering Karak as they raced just over the floor. He found that squeezing with his thighs was the best way to tell Karak how fast or slow he wanted to go. The faster he went, the more his stomach churned. Sweat poured down his face and back, soaking his shirt. His hands were slippery with it and his heart was racing. Despite this, he whooped.

How could something be so exhausting, so terrifying, and yet so fun at the same time? Abel had never felt anything like this before. It was the scariest kind of freedom, right on the edge of danger. He couldn't imagine how dragon riders ever got used to it; he was kind of *afraid* of ever getting used to it. All he knew was, he wanted to keep going.

"This is AWESOME!" he yelled as he buzzed over the machine where Ally, Topher, and Roa stood, then turned again, weaving between the catwalks in a loop. Karak burst back through the huge warehouse to take another high-speed run at the wall. Abel realized he'd never *really* known what the word "awesome" meant until now. Though he was feeling a lot more than *some* awe.

After a few more loops of the warehouse and factory, Ally's voice came back over the earbuds. "Okay, dragon rider, bring him in for a landing."

"Ep ep!" Abel barked, like a real dragon cadet.

"In the kin we say 'savvy,'" Roa told him over the earbuds. Abel felt a momentary sting of embarrassment, both for not knowing that and for never having heard Roa say it before. It reminded him how they'd kept this whole other life secret from him.

For how long? he wondered. Was growing up just realizing that everyone you loved hid pieces of themselves from you? And that you, in turn, learned which pieces to hide from them? He'd never been good at hiding things, which was why he always lost cards at DrakoTek. Maybe the reason adults didn't play games like DrakoTek was because their whole lives were already games of strategy and deception. The world was the deck, and your life was the hand you were dealt. Growing up was learning the rules as you went along and hoping your hand didn't run out of cards before you got good at the game.

"Abel, focus!" Roa's voice cut into his thoughts. His attention snapped back just as he buzzed over the machines and circled the entire warehouse again. He'd totally tuned out again, but his body had kept steering. That was good to know . . . but he had to do better at paying attention. A distracted dragon rider would become a dead dragon rider pretty quick.

"Ep ep!" he said back. "I mean . . . savvy!"

On the next loop, he leaned forward so that his cheek was pressed against the dragon. Then he squeezed his legs tighter and slowly released them. The dragon descended, claws sparking off the concrete floor. The smooth glide was replaced by teeth-cracking bounces as Karak came to a panting stop. He towered over Roa, Ally, and Topher. He opened his mouth wide, like he was about to blast them all with a ball of fire.

"AHHH!" Topher yelled, and tried to hide behind his mop again.

Abel was still pulling back on Karak's spiky spine. He let go, shouting, "Whoa there! Whoa!"

Karak let the flame die in his throat. Smoke puffed from his nose. He settled down to let Abel off with a sparkling sigh of disappointment.

"Woo!" Abel said as soon as his feet hit the ground. "That was awesome! What's next?"

"Don't get cocky," Ally said. "That's enough for today."

"But I was only up there for like five minutes!" Abel objected.

"It's been three and a half hours," Topher grumbled.

"Shh," Ally silenced him again.

Abel pulled out his phone and looked at the clock.

"Time flies when you're flying," Roa observed.

"Roa, check the dragon's injury," Ally instructed. "Make sure your stitches from last night held." Roa scurried over to study the dragon's wing joint, and Ally turned back to Abel. "Remember to stretch," she told him. "You're going to be sore." Then she pointed at a trough of water and a tied-up goat. "Once Roa is finished, you will feed your dragon, then clean it thoroughly and go home."

His stomach sank looking at the goat and at the trough.

"It's not all speed and glory when you're responsible for another creature," Ally said. "Care for your dragon properly, and it'll care for you. Also, when you get home, check your email. There will be reading assigned."

"Cleaning *and* reading? When do I learn how to battle?"

Ally shook her head. "When you prove you're ready and not a moment before." She gave him and Roa each a curt nod, then turned to leave. She snapped her fingers, and Topher scurried after her. "I swear, boy, you are the laziest, most obnoxious child I have ever met. I understand why your family sent you out of the house to work for me, I just don't understand why the Thunder Wings would punish *me* with you."

She kept haranguing Topher all the way up the catwalk stairs and across the factory. Abel went from almost feeling bad for Topher to actually feeling bad for him. Topher had even less choice to be here than Abel did, and he didn't get to ride a dragon.

"See you at sunrise!" Ally called down from the exit door. "And, Abel, tomorrow, *please* remember to wear deodorant." She made a sour face as she left. Abel sniffed himself and flinched. If he could weaponize that smell, he'd never lose a battle.

THE DAYS WENT ON LIKE that for the rest of the week. Abel trudged out in the early morning to fly across town with the bleary-eyed shift workers and the blearier-eyed up-all-nighters. Then he'd slip into the warehouse with his keycard as quickly as he could for the day's training. Thunder Wings goons in their Thunder Wings colors leaned on the wall outside the warehouse, keeping watch.

"Look at Abel, hope he's able, or they won't give his grave a label," one of the goons sang at him. Jusif was his name. He was high school age but didn't go to school. He seemed to spend most of his time leaning against the wall sucking on ginger candy or sitting on a stool and making one of the other gangsters trim his hair. He kept the back and sides of his head neatly shaved but had a mop of red curls on top that he obsessively styled. On the back of his neck, right at the base of his skull, he'd tattooed the symbol of the Thunder Wings. Abel wondered what his parents must've thought of that. Then again, for kinners like him, the kin probably was his parents.

"You want to come inside and sing me that song?" Abel asked. "I bet Karak would *love* to hear it."

Jusif's tough-guy act fell away. He laughed nervously.

"I have an . . . uh . . . appointment . . . for my haircut!" he said, and disappeared around the corner to gamble over

DrakoTek with the other Thunder Wings. They never wanted to come inside. They weren't afraid of Abel, but Karak terrified them.

Karak terrified Abel too, but he and the dragon were also becoming friends. Though he did occasionally worry that they were becoming friends the way fire made friends with fuel.

"Good, you're here," Roa greeted him inside. They were wearing a jumpsuit in Thunder Wings colors. Ally was in a matching one. Topher was wearing the same clothes he'd had on yesterday, looking sullen. Ally sent him outside to see if Jusif or the others needed anything. "And so I don't have to look at you today," she said.

In front of Abel, there was all kinds of big equipment laid out on a tarp. A huge metal dragon helmet. Big plates of dragon armor. There were battery packs, and hoses attached to tanks, and barbed-wire netting, and every assortment of spikes and bombs and nasty-looking devices.

These were definitely not things city hall gave out licenses for.

"Is that *battle* gear?!" Abel couldn't suppress a grin. He'd spent days flying in circles, spinning upside down until he made himself sick, and then doing it again after he got sick. Then more feeding and cleaning. It would be hard to say dragon training was dull, but he was ready to get to the cool stuff.

"It is battle gear," his instructor said. "But not for you. *That's* for you." She pointed at a heap of leather and metal all tangled up right next to Karak, who had added it to his hoard. "This morning you only have one task. Put the saddle on your dragon."

Abel looked from his teacher to Roa and back again.

"That's it?" He crossed over to the hoard, scrambling up the cans until he was at the saddle harness. He grabbed on to one of its big metal rings, looking up at Karak. "This won't be too bad. It's just some buckles and straps and—oof!"

It weighed a lot more than he thought it would. Abel heaved and pulled so hard his face turned red and he felt muscles straining that he didn't even know he had. He looked over at Roa, but Ally stopped them from helping him.

"This is impossible," he groaned. "Won't I have a ground crew for this? What about Topher?"

"Topher is my intern, not yours," Ally said. "And a dragon rider who can't saddle his dragon is hardly a dragon rider at all. You rushed to the harness without remembering your OODA loop. You skipped right to the *da*."

"I did what?" he groaned; then he remembered.

Observe.

Orient.

Decide.

Act.

Abel had *acted* before *oo'ing*.

He let go of the strap he was holding and looked at the harness—*observed* it. The saddle part was shaped to fit over the base of the dragon's neck. It had handles on the front and back for him to hold on to. There was a ring on a ball bearing to clip his safety harness to so he could move freely around the saddle. There was a big loop that buckled around the dragon's neck and some straps that went to the back of the saddle attached to a series of loops for the dragon's tail. All the loops were attached to strong steel thread ropes and reins. There were metal stirrups for his feet and a few other rings where he'd be able to hang supply boxes and battery packs and weapons system controls.

It was a lot of stuff, but it wasn't nearly as tangled as it had first seemed and all of it was designed to be lightweight. Why was he having such trouble pulling it?

Then he saw. One loop of metal from one of the tail controls was resting right by Karak's front foot. The dragon had slipped a claw through it, holding it in place. No matter how hard Abel pulled, he'd never get it out of the dragon's grip.

When he looked up at Karak, he thought he saw that draconic smirk. "Are you *messing* with me, you ten-ton twerp?!"

He looked back at Ally and Roa, who were laughing.

"I can't believe my own dragon pranked me," Abel shouted. "And that my teacher and best friend helped!"

"We're kinners," Ally called over to him. "Why do all of this if we can't have a little fun?"

Karak's body quivered, and sparks crackled from his nose. He was laughing too, but he let go of the saddle.

He'd *observed*, so now Abel had to *orient* himself, which meant pulling the saddle into the best position he could, laying out all the straps how he thought they should go, and then *deciding* how best to put it on his dragon.

He stared at it for a long while.

"Is there no instruction manual?" he called.

"There is!" Roa called back. "I've read it, but Ally says you have to figure this out for yourself."

"Ugh, fine!" Abel hated that thing teachers did where they already knew the right answer but they wanted to watch you squirm to figure it out anyway. It took him the better part of an hour to get to the end of his OODA loop and *act*.

And then he put the saddle on backward.

It took four more tries before he got it right. Twice he put it on so tight that Karak almost fried him, and once he put it on so loose that it—and he—fell off as soon he climbed on.

When he finally got it on right and sat proudly on the Sunrise Reaper's back, cheering for himself (because no one else was cheering for him), Ally ordered him to take it off again.

Then she blindfolded him.

"You need to be able to do it a lot faster and in the dark," she said. "Get to it."

The sun was setting by the time he'd gotten the hang of it. Now he could put the saddle on perfectly on the first try, in the dark, without making a sound. He was exhausted, but felt like a real dragon rider.

He smelled like one too.

• • •

After Karak was fed and cleaned again, Topher came in to mop. It looked like Jusif and the others had given him a haircut, and not a good one, but Abel had enough problems of his own without borrowing trouble from Topher.

Abel also had his eyes on the battle equipment laid out on the tarp.

"Do we have time to try that stuff today?" he asked Ally. "I didn't even get to fly."

"Being a rider isn't just about flying," Ally said. "You are responsible for another creature . . . and its equipment. Most of what you do will be feeding, cleaning, and repairing."

"But . . . I could fly a little, right? So Karak doesn't forget how?"

"He won't," Ally said. "He's a dragon."

"But I might?" Abel tried. "I need a lot of practice, right? Or I could learn a new move?"

"No new moves," Ally said. "You aren't ready."

"But I am!" Abel said. "Look how good I got at the saddle!"

Ally raised an eyebrow, thinking. Then gave him a curt nod. "Fine," she said. "I'll teach you one new maneuver. Mount up."

Abel ran back to the dragon. "One more time in the air, buddy?" he said eagerly.

Karak, full-bellied and clean-scaled, grunted, but he let Abel put the saddle back on again and climb aboard.

"Another thing!" Ally called out to him. "You'll need this from now on."

She tossed him a sleek black helmet that sparkled a little, just like Karak's scales. It had a black faceplate and night vision capabilities and even a little fan to keep him from overheating. The helmet was so cool it almost made Abel forget that it was for keeping his brains from being turned into pudding.

When they were off the ground, Ally gave her instructions. "I want you to fly straight for the far wall. When you're ten wingspans away, draw a spiral pattern with your fingers on your dragon's neck so he knows what you want. Wait to make sure he understands, then pull hard to the left, lean to the right, and bring the dragon in to swirl around itself. This move is called the whirlpool. It's a way to turn without your opponent being able to predict where you'll go. You can break from the twirl at any point in any direction."

"Got it!" Abel said. He squeezed his legs to speed the dragon up, flapping straight for the wall. He had to guess when they were ten wingspans out, because he wasn't good at knowing how big a wingspan was, but then he traced the spiral pattern, yanked the reins, and leaned. Karak tucked his wings, curling his neck toward his tail, and twirled.

It worked! They fell into a spinning dive!

It worked too well . . . They were spinning really, really fast!

Abel felt the g-forces pull him sideways, then pull him even harder. The walls of the warehouse whirled around him, and his body lifted from the saddle. He'd forgotten to clip himself into the safety harness!

"Whoa, Karak!" he yelled, pulling the reins, but the force of the spin was too strong. He couldn't stop! Round and round Karak spun, dropping toward the floor with every rotation. He was also speeding up, and the force pulling on Abel made him pull the reins harder, which made Karak spin faster.

"Let go!" Roa yelled in his ear. "Bail!"

"I can't!" he yelled back. The world blurred around him. His body lifted off the dragon's back, legs flying out from under him, pulling him away into open air. Only his hands on the reins kept him from spinning off and dashing his brains. His vision started to go red, then white, and narrowed to a pinpoint.

"Slooooow dooooooown!" he yelled, but Karak couldn't hear him.

He was about to pass out when . . . CRASH!

Karak's huge body smashed into the floor. It cracked with such force that a tidal wave of broken concrete rolled over one of the big can-making machines, burying it. Abel was flung off in the other direction, hurtling head over feet across the floor to a hard stop against the brick wall. If he hadn't been wearing a helmet, he'd have been killed. As it was, he'd be bruised and scraped and sore.

And now he knew what bricks tasted like.

"Ughh," he groaned, which was the only way he could know he was still alive. Being dead surely didn't sting as much as this. Then a jolt of adrenaline hit him. Karak's body had taken most of the impact of the crash. It had probably saved Abel's life.

He bolted up to his feet and ran over to the dragon, who lay in a crater of broken concrete and sparking wires.

"Are you okay?" He wrapped his arms around Karak's snout. The dragon looked at him with one eye and grunted a blast of steam, then stood ponderously and trudged back to the other machine room to lie on his hoard of cans.

Abel limped after him, to find Roa checking the dragon for wounds. "He's not hurt," they said. "Dragons can take a lot of impact . . . but you're a mess."

"Thanks," Abel grunted.

Ally stood with her arms crossed, eyeing Abel. "What did you learn?"

"Always wear your helmet?" he suggested.

"And?"

"There are some moves I'm not ready for," he said.

She nodded. "Good. So when I tell you you aren't ready, what will you do?"

"Listen to you." He looked at his feet.

"Precisely," she said. Then she told him to help her move the battle gear out to the loading dock.

"So if this stuff isn't for me and Karak," Abel asked, "who is it for?"

"Me," Ally said. "And *my* dragon."

Ally tapped her earpiece, and the cargo doors at the far end of the warehouse creaked open, letting in the gleaming red light of dusk. Jusif and a few of the other Thunder Wings came in carrying a long chain over their shoulders. At the end of it was a huge wheeled cage the size of a parade float, covered with an equally huge sheet. Ally pulled the sheet off. Inside the cage stood a grand Yellow Stinger dragon. Its snout and tail were covered in long barbs, the biggest as tall as Abel himself.

The dragon looked down at Ally, opened its mouth, and shrieked so loudly even Karak buried his head under a wing.

The dragon was furious. Ally smiled.

"I did like you said," Jusif told her, his voice shuddering with fear. "Showed her a box of jewels, then took it away. She's madder than a pangolin put into a pocketbook."

"Good." Ally smiled and reached through the bars of the cage to pat the dragon's huge foot. "Then she's ready for tonight's battle."

"Battle?" Abel whispered to Roa.

"There's been a challenge from the Red Talons," Roa said. "You and Karak aren't ready, so Ally's going to fly Zoonia against their dragon. And *we'll* be her ground crew."

Topher bounced on the balls of his feet. He was so excited. "We're gonna get to see a *real* kin battle! Tonight!"

"I already called your parents and told them you'd be home

late," Ally shouted over to Abel. "Now get changed so you're in our colors." Jusif threw a puffy jumpsuit at him. It had the Thunder Wings lightning-dragon symbol sewn in reflective purple thread across the entire back and stitched onto sleeve patches.

"If you do well," Justif said, "we might just get our symbol inked onto your neck." He laughed, then looked up at Karak and changed his tone. "I mean, like . . . if . . . er . . . you wanted it."

"You're *so* tough, Jusif," Roa mocked him. "Just make sure when we're out there you keep a lookout for me. That's your job, right? To look out, not to chatter like a brainless bone spur."

"You do your job, I'll do mine," Jusif said. "But what's No Label Abel gonna do? We don't want deadweight on the team."

"He's gonna watch and learn," Ally interrupted them. "And try to keep from losing his head, like the last guy who had that jumpsuit."

Abel's chest tightened.

"He didn't *literally* lose his head," Roa reassured him.

"Yeah," Jusif laughed. "It was still partway attached!"

14

THE GLASS FLATS CIRCLED THE edge of Drakopolis, beyond the districts of skyscrapers and apartment blocks, past the factories and warehouses and the high-rise farms.

Once, the Flats were a great sand desert. Before that, they were a lush wilderness, or so the stories said. But back in the Before, when the dragons were wild and there were no people in the world, the unruly monsters of the sky feasted on the animals and the insects and the trees and the grasses. They glutted themselves on everything they saw until there was nothing left and the wilderness became sand. Then they began to devour each other. As they fought and bled and fought some more, their fiery breath burned the sand to glass, creating a smooth and lifeless waste. The dragons nearly drove themselves to extinction.

The few survivors, mad and starved and surrounded by an endless desert of colorful glass, would have died off too, if they hadn't been saved by the humans who arrived—the stories never said where the humans came from or what they'd been up to before.

The humans founded the city of Drakopolis and pacified the dragons—the stories never explained how—and they built a home where all would have plenty of food and shelter. Humanity saved the dragons and made them useful, and by being useful, the dragons found peace.

Dragons must be given purpose, the stories said, *so they don't fall to warring again. They must be given jobs and kept busy serving humanity*, the stories said, *for their own safety.*

So the stories said.

It was all a long time ago, but even now when it came time for dragons to fight, they went back to the desert, back to the Glass Flats. That was where all kin battles started.

It was just after sunset when Ally and the Thunder Wings arrived at the place. Dark but not so late that the city behind them wasn't bustling. People were just heading home from work, or going out to dinner, or finishing up practice or play rehearsal. Abel's mother was probably just clocking out at the feed plant and starting the long bus flight home.

The lights of the city bent and shimmered in the colorful glass all around where Abel stood. The sight was breathtaking. The starlight up above made him think of Karak, back in the warehouse. He could see the swirls of distant galaxies, the whirl and streak of shooting stars, constellations he could never see from his window in the city.

"Wow," he said.

"Yeah," Roa agreed.

"Savvy," Topher sighed. Not even he could be sarcastic in the face of the entire universe twirling above them.

"Hey, eyes down," Jusif snapped at them. "You're the ground crew, not the stare-at-the-stars crew." He grunted at Topher. "And you. Go help Olus with the supplies before I make dragon snacks out of you."

Topher scurried over to the Thunder Wings leader, who was sorting all kinds of tools and supplies and weapons systems to enhance their dragon. It was like a real-life stack of DrakoTek cards.

"Get me the hex wrench, you slobbering salamander," Olus snapped at Topher. "Unless you want to me to use your teeth on this bolt!"

Poor Topher scurried from Olus to the tool chest, rummaging frantically.

"Our job is to fix Ally's equipment, patch up any wounds we can, and keep Zoonia in flying shape," Jusif explained. "Roa, you're on medical, obviously. I'm the lookout. I warn her of incoming trouble. Olus is the Fix-It, doing repairs and upgrades when Ally comes back to the pit."

"Your leader is your Fix-It?" Abel asked, watching the kin leader scold Topher about the size of the wrench he'd brought back.

"Thunder Wings value smarts above all else," Roa said. "Some kins idolize their dragon riders, but we admire our Fix-Its and our Healers. That's why they're letting you fly Karak with, like, no training, but I have to apprentice for years to be a dragon vet."

"It's not *no* training," Abel corrected them. "And it's Karak letting me fly, not the Thunder Wings."

"Right, of course," Roa said. Abel suspected his friend was humoring him.

They'd outfitted the Yellow Stinger with armor and weapons. The spikes on her tail were now tipped with impact grenades. She had on a helmet with a targeting laser and loops of wire that went from the helmet's base to the back of her jaw so that her breath weapon was calibrated to the laser for targeting.

Yellow Stingers breathed fire, the most common for all the dragons, but it wasn't as hot as a lot of others. So the Thunder Wings had designed a kind of mask for the end of Zoonia's snout. When the flame passed through the mask, it hit a chemical that was like syrup. Whatever the dragon hit with a fireball, the flame would stick to and burn slow and hot, smoldering for a long, long time. It could melt armor. Abel shuddered to think what it could do to a person.

Just then, a wide-winged shadow passed over them. The jagged shape of a dragon blotted out the starlight. It circled in for a landing on the Glass Flats with a clattering of claws. Then, rearing back on its hind legs, it let out a roar.

The Red Talons challenger had arrived on a Ruby Widow Maker.

The bright red dragon had red armor covering its belly, and there were missile tubes at the base of each of its wings. Its forepaws had flamethrowers mounted to the backs of special dragon-sized gloves and its back paws had huge blades over its talons that doubled their length. Its helmet was just as red as its scales but had a smooth rainbow glass visor that covered its eyes completely, to protect them during the battle. Widow Makers were gem dragons, and their breath weapon fired razor-sharp gem fragments. The gem shrapnel could easily ricochet and hurt the dragon, which was why you couldn't play any Widow Maker in DrakoTek unless you also had an equipment card with some kind of eye covering. They were one of the few dragons whose power was so strong they could hurt themselves with it.

The rider was dressed from head to toe in red armor, except for a fully mirrored helmet. He jumped down from the saddle and took it off in one smooth motion. It was Sax, the kinner who'd torn up Abel's apartment. He smiled at Abel with yellow teeth.

"Your sister stole something that belongs to *us*," he shouted. "And now it's fallen into Thunder Wings hands. Return it."

"We return nothing," Olus bellowed on Abel's behalf. "And I'm insulted they'd send *you* to fly. Where's your boss?"

"Red Talons leaders have more important things to do than fight over scraps," Sax answered.

Olus spat on the ground. "Dismantle this fool."

"Savvy," Ally replied with a bow, then turned to Sax. "Terms?"

"We want the Sunrise Reaper," Sax said.

"No," Ally said. "You only win the dragon that battles. That's the way. Winner takes the loser's dragon."

"I want to battle the Sunrise Reaper, then!" Sax said.

"The rider isn't trained yet," Ally said. "You battle me."

"Okay, fine. Our terms are this," Sax said. "*When* we win, we get to battle the Sunrise Reaper next week, ready or not."

"And if you lose?"

Sax laughed so hard he nearly wheezed. "*If* I lose, you get Zuk." He pointed at his bright red dragon. "And . . . we'll forgive the boy's sister for her theft."

Abel's heart leapt. Maybe this could solve all his family's problems *and* he wouldn't even have to battle.

"His sister's a Sky Knight," Olus scoffed. "Why would we want to help her?" Abel's heart sank, but Ally looked over at him and gave a thumbs-up. Olus nodded at her. "Fine," he grunted at Sax. "For the boy's sake."

Abel smiled.

"Don't be too happy about that bet," Olus whispered to him. "We bail your sister out of her trouble for you, then you're going to owe us, just like your friend Topher does."

"But he's not my—" Abel started.

"Kindness always has a price in this city, kid," Ally cut him off. "Get used to it."

Abel didn't want to get used to that kind of kindness. Real kindness wasn't a trade you made; it was gift you gave. He didn't like the kinner version of kindness at all.

A small shape darted from the darkness between two distant floodlights on the border with the city. It grew larger as it raced toward them across the smooth glass.

Abel tensed. "Is that the Dragon's Eye?" he gasped, terrified not only of being carted off to Windlee Prison, but having his parents find out that he and Roa *and* their teacher had been lying to them. He didn't want to let them down. They had enough trouble.

"No, the Dragon's Eye flies wyverns," Roa said. "*That* is Fitz."

The shape grew larger and larger as Fitz, the owner of Chimera's All-Night Coffee + Comics, sped across the Flats on the back of a colorful serpentine dragon. The creature had a long, thin body, four strong scale-covered legs, and a mane of thick white hair that flowed in the breeze. The dragon came to swirling stop in between the two teams, and Fitz hopped down from his dragon's back with surprising gracefulness for a man of his size.

Fitz was a legend around the city. Everyone thought he'd been in a kin before, but no one knew which one. He had tattoos for all the major kins on the knuckles of one hand, and the word "UNITY" on the knuckles of his other. He had tattoos that told stories up and down his arms, some from the other side of the Glass Flats, where he'd traveled in the Dragon Corps, and some from Windlee Prison, where he'd volunteered as a nurse in the hospital. He had one tooth made out of gleaming dragon glass, and it shimmered whenever he let out one of his thunderous laughs, which he did often.

"Sorry I'm late," Fitz said. "We had a story time at the shop. You would not believe how many requests a group of three-year-olds can make! But I brought leftover donuts! Anyone want one?"

He reached for one of his saddlebags, where Abel saw a bright pink box peeking out. It made his mouth water.

"I'll take one," Topher said, but Olus slapped his hand away and made him sort the tools alphabetically.

"This is a battle, not snack time," Sax snarled. "Get on with it!"

"Of course." Fitz bowed. "For the record, I know nothing about any of this and am only out here on my evening ride." As he climbed back up onto his dragon, he caught Abel's eye, and his beaming smile tripped into a frown. He obviously hadn't been expecting to see Abel. But he cleared his throat, pasted his happy expression back on, and spoke to everyone in his usual booming voice. "CHALLENGER! SURRENDER YOUR HOARD!"

Sax, as the challenger from the Red Talons, stepped forward with a large token about the size of a trash can lid. It was covered in gems and jewels and looked like it might've been solid gold. The Red Talons' emblem was made out of rubies on one side and diamonds on the other. It was definitely precious. It also looked heavy.

"Dragons, to your lairs!" Fitz shouted. Each of the pilots scurried back onto their dragons, which were waiting in the spray-painted circles on the ground, each kin's symbol at the center. "As usual, I will hide the hoard on a rooftop within the city limits and send up this signal when it's placed."

Fitz pulled back on the reins of his dragon gently. It tilted its head back to the sky and opened its mouth. A ball of purple flame formed at the back of its throat, and then it shot straight up in a gleaming tower of fire. The flare turned into a great round ball of rainbow flame, which fell as colorful sparks. "Look to the horizon," Fitz said. He gave his dragon a tug on the reins and shouted, "Ep ep!"

Two thin purple wings erupted from the dragon's sides, and it leapt into the air, flapping away with astonishing speed. Soon, Fitz disappeared into the city skyline.

Now they had to wait. No one could take off before the signal, but once it came, the goal was to find the hoard somewhere in the city before the other team did, grab it, and get back your team's starting circle. That ended the battle. Whoever got the hoard to their circle first won.

Each team had a ground crew who could give advice and instruction, do repairs, and offer quick healing care. Only the designated rider and their battle dragon could participate in the battle, though. Any other dragons interfering was cheating and an automatic forfeit. Also, the ground crews weren't allowed to beat each other up.

Those were about the only rules.

"How long does it take for Fitz to hide the hoard?" Abel asked. "And why Fitz?"

"He's the only person in the entire city that everyone trusts," Roa said. "But that doesn't mean everyone respects him. The kin have spies watching where he goes, so he has to be sneaky. He can't be seen placing the hoard, but he also can't send the signal from the same place he hid it. He's really good. No one has ever managed to see him hide it."

"Do the Thunder Wings spy on him too?"

"Of course." Roa shrugged. "We value knowledge. What are spies but collectors of knowledge?"

"That's cheating," Abel said.

"Can't cheat if there are no rules against it," Jusif added. "Relax. This is gonna be fun!"

"It's a deadly and illegal dragon battle," Abel reminded him.

"Right!" Jusif pumped his fist "Like I said, fun! Hey, Topher the gopher, get me a soda."

Abel frowned, while Topher glumly brought Drake-Cola from the cooler, then retreated back to Olus's side. He looked miserable. Abel didn't want to end up like him, trapped as a servant to these vicious kinners. He looked back at Roa, unsure what he was supposed to do now.

"It's my first battle too," they said. "I *am* kind of excited. It's beautiful out here, isn't it?"

Abel looked up at the stars and then down at the way they gleamed off the Glass Flats. He thrilled at the thought of Karak's sparkling wings spread wide out here, flying free and open, not crammed into the warehouse. The air smelled cleaner too, none of that mix of sweat, metal, and dragon dung that filled the city. And from this distance, the city itself looked beautiful. He'd never seen it from the outside before. This far away, you couldn't tell where the dirt was, or where the buildings were run-down and the landing platforms cracked. From here, it looked like a magical place to grow up. He felt a swell of gratitude that he was lucky enough to have been born in it, to be alive and young and caught up in an adventure. It was beautiful and scary, and yeah . . . maybe Jusif was right. It was fun.

"Hey, focus!" Olus shouted, snapping him to attention. "Look for the signal!"

A moment later, he saw it. A ball of purple fire hovered in the air, then burst into rainbow sparks.

The Red Talons' Widow Maker dragon was off the ground first. Ally on her Yellow Stinger launched a heartbeat later, screeching into the sky.

A blast of thick orange smoke shot from a backward-facing cannon on the Widow Maker's side. The Yellow Stinger had to dodge it in a corkscrew spin, which slowed her down, giving the Red Talons team a chance to turn and snap at the other dragon. Talon clashed with metal, throwing bright sparks into the night. The dragons snarled and thrashed, then broke apart on the way back to the city line. Ally slowed so her dragon was behind the Red Talons'. The Yellow Stinger fired a blast of flame from her mouth that smashed directly into the Widow Maker's armored belly. The Widow Maker roared and turned to get away, veering in a new direction. Ally accelerated her dragon and gained speed, veering in the opposite direction.

It's a race, a heist, and a duel, Abel remembered. It took speed, smarts, and power. It looked like Ally and her dragon had all three. *When it's my turn*, he thought, *will I?*

The two dragons disappeared into the bright city lights, and just like that, Abel's first kin battle had begun.

15

"**KEEP YOUR EYE ON THEIR** dragon," Roa instructed. "We need to see where it searches, if it finds anything, and if it turns to attack Ally." They handed Abel some high-tech binoculars that had night vision buttons and infrared buttons and even a button that could look through buildings to see the unique energy dragons gave off.

"Don't drop those!" Olus shouted over at Abel. "They cost more than any of your lives."

Abel held them like he was holding a dragon's egg. They focused automatically when he raised them to his eyes, which was pretty cool, and he saw the Ruby Widow Maker like it was still right in front of him. It was swooping in lazy arcs over a neighborhood at the edge of the city. Not like it was searching, but like it was waiting.

"Red Talons only love power," Roa said. "They always attack right at the start, trying to intimidate the other team . . . but really it's so they can install a tracker."

They pointed to Ally's dragon, flying in a search pattern over the rooftops of a mid-city neighborhood. Through the binoculars Abel saw the pulsing device that the Red Talons pilot had secretly attached when their dragons collided.

"Ally, you've got a tracker on your belly," Roa said to their earpiece. Then, to Abel, "Keep your eye on *their* dragon, not ours."

Abel scanned the sky for the Widow Maker again, but he kept looking back at Ally as she climbed the rings around her saddle harness and went underneath her dragon in midair to remove the tracker. The moment it fell away, Sax spurred his dragon to speed up and begin the search for himself.

"Nice try!" Jusif yelled at the Red Talons ground crew, who returned his comment with a rude gesture.

The Widow Maker disappeared between two tall farm buildings. Abel pressed a button to switch over to Dragonview Mode. The buildings became outlines, and he saw the shapes of hundreds of the dragons flying between and around them, highlighted in bright green outlines. He pressed a bunch of buttons, and the binoculars automatically labeled the breeds of every dragon he saw, which helped him find the two he was after. There was even a button that locked on them and made their outlines brighter so he didn't lose them among the taxis and haulers and buses of the city at night.

He watched the Widow Maker zig and zag over the ground, then turn sharply upward, flying over a district of apartment buildings.

"Update." Ally's voice came over his earbuds.

"Uh . . ." Abel said. "Their dragon is by some apartment buildings."

Ally's voice came back clipped and impatient, like when Topher gave wrong answers to easy questions in class. "Are they moving like they've found anything? Or are they headed toward me?"

"I don't know," Abel said, feeling foolish. "They're kind of just . . . flying."

"Abel, use your brain!" his teacher snapped. "What do you know about them?"

"Well, the pilot, Sax, is a jerk."

"We're all jerks," Jusif sneered. "That's kind of the point."

"I mean, Sax is such a jerk that he threatens to beat up kids," Abel said. "I bet he's not really looking for the hoard. He's just waiting for you to find it so he can steal it." He lowered his binoculars and glanced over at the Red Talons ground crew. They were talking to Sax on their own earpieces but also watching Abel.

"Good," Ally said. "That probably *is* his strategy."

"Or he just wants you to think he's not looking while he actually is looking so you don't notice when he finds it," Roa said.

"You're overthinking it," Ally told them. "That can be worse than not thinking at all."

Roa grunted, and Abel tried to stifle his smirk. It wasn't often he got a compliment from a teacher and Roa didn't.

"I'm making my move," Ally announced. "Savvy?"

"Savvy," Olus replied.

"That means she thinks she'd found the hoard," Roa told Abel.

"Incoming!" Olus shouted. "Abel, do your job!"

Abel looked back through the binoculars, but he couldn't find the Widow Maker for a moment. Then he saw it speeding over the high rooftops of a warehouse district, aiming straight for Ally's Yellow Stinger, which was circling a school building.

"What happens if one team disables the other's dragon?" Abel asked. "Or, like, kills the rider?"

"Then they've got all the time in the world to find the hoard," Roa said. "They still have to find it to win."

"Even if the other side is—"

"Dead," Jusif interjected. "Yep. Makes it a whole lot easier, though."

Roa shrugged. "It's a strategy the Red Talons like. Kill the other side's rider, then hunt for the treasure in peace."

"That's brutal."

"That's how it happens in all the ancient stories," Roa said. "Knights killing dragons for their treasure. Dragons killing knights for theirs. At least this makes it a fair fight . . . kind of. And it's my job to make sure our dragon doesn't get killed. Dragons are tough creatures, and I'm good at healing them. Anyway, when you win, you usually win the other side's dragon. No one wants to kill their own prize, so dragons rarely die in these battles."

"But what about the riders?" Abel asked.

"Yeah, that does happen . . ." Roa shrugged. "But Ally will be fine; relax."

"Relax? Now?" Abel shook his head and watched as the two dragons closed in on each other, breath weapons ready.

The Widow Maker was above the Yellow Stinger. It fired first, blasting out a stream of glittery gem shards toward Ally. She spun her dragon in a corkscrew, using her armored belly to block the attack, which made Roa and Abel wince. The armor was strong, but not impenetrable, and a dragon's belly was their weak spot.

The Yellow Stinger roared, but it kept twirling and escaped the attack. A lot of the shards missed completely, instead blasting holes into an office building behind them. The Yellow Stinger flicked her tail as they passed below the Widow Maker, and two of the grenades on the ends of her spikes launched. They exploded and sent the big red dragon off course, smashing hard into the wall of a neighboring skyscraper. Sax regained control and dove for the top of a tall shopping complex, smashing off two landing platforms from the side of a building on his way.

Abel really hoped that no one was working late in these buildings. A kin battle was dangerous enough for the riders; he'd hate to think of the innocent bystanders.

"Oatmeal!" one of the Red Talons ground crew shouted, which made Abel and the other Thunder Wings look in their direction.

"Why did he just shout 'oatmeal'?" Abel asked.

"It must be a code word," Roa said.

"For what?" Abel asked, but he got his answer when the Widow Maker charged at Ally and her dragon again.

"It means they know Ally found the hoard . . ." Roa said.

"On your six!" Jusif warned as the big red dragon closed in. The yellow dragon weaved from side to side and slashed her spiked tail through the air to launch grenades. The flame-throwers on the Widow Maker's claws blasted the grenades before they could explode; then it fired a jagged shard with its gem breath. Ally ducked and turned her dragon sharply at the same instant.

But not fast enough.

The gem grazed one of Zoonia's forelegs. The yellow dragon yelped so loud they could hear it all the way from where they stood on the Glass Flats.

"Her leg's cut!" Roa cried, staring through their own binoculars. "She's bleeding!"

"Ally or her dragon?" Abel asked.

"Her dragon, duh," Jusif snapped at him. "If the gem had hit her, she'd be falling from the sky in a thousand pieces."

"I need a refill on tail bombs," Ally said. Abel was still imagining his teacher being shredded by jagged jewels somewhere over the city. "Before I make another run. Keep your eye on them, Abel."

She turned her dragon back toward the Glass Flats. The Widow Maker broke off pursuit, going on the hunt for the hoard while Ally retreated for repairs and healing. It circled the area where she'd been flying, trying to see what she had seen.

The Yellow Stinger clattered in for a landing, kicking up shards of smooth glass as she slowed. Olus leapt onto the side of her harness before she'd even stopped moving. He had a big tool belt on, and in moments he was attaching new grenades to the tail, hammering out dents in the armor, and using a small welding torch to patch holes, yelling at Topher all the while to hand him supplies. It was mesmerizing to watch him work.

Meanwhile, Roa knelt beneath the dragon with the same eagerness they brought to giving answers in school. They were using big tweezers with some kind of motor and battery system to pull gruesome fragments of red glass out of the dragon's yellow leg. Ally hopped down and came over to Abel.

"What are you learning?" she asked him.

"That these battles are brutal," Abel said.

"Dragons are born brutal," Ally said. "We domesticated them to haul our buses and power our factories, but they're fighters by nature. These battles give them a chance to be themselves. Don't go weak-kneed about it now. Tell me what you learned about tactics and strategy."

"The Red Talons dragon is all about violence," Abel said. "But the team doesn't know where to look or even how to search." He pointed to the distant skyline, where their dragon was sweeping back and forth, scanning the same landscape over and over but coming up short. The Red Talons ground crew were whispering and gesturing and arguing with each other. "They've got power but no smarts."

Ally nodded. "And we've got smarts but not enough power to defeat their dragon. So what do we do?"

"Uh . . . outsmart them?" Abel said.

"Exactly." Ally clapped him on the back, then mounted her dragon once more.

"Clear!" Olus shouted, leaping down as he tightened the last new grenade in place.

"Clear!" Roa said, scrambling out from underneath the dragon, who had already started running for a takeoff toward the city again. But not back to where they'd been searching. Ally was heading somewhere else entirely. Why? How would going to the wrong place outsmart the Red Talons?

Oh.

Abel realized what she was up to. The Red Talons were cheaters. They were going to let her do the hard work of finding the hoard, then just take it—like a cheater on the test just takes your answers. How did you foil someone copying your answers?

You choose the wrong answer on purpose, then change it when they aren't looking.

"Fiddlesticks!" Abel yelled.

Roa and Olus looked at him. Jusif kept his binoculars pointed to the city but grumbled back at him. "What are yelling nonsense for?"

"I want *them* to think *we* have a code word," Abel whispered into the microphone so they could only hear him through their earbuds . . . and so that his teacher could hear how helpful he was being. "I want them to think she's found the hoard where she's heading this time."

Roa grinned as the Red Talons ground crew muttered into their own earbuds, stealing glances in Abel's direction. It was working.

The Widow Maker raced after Ally. The Yellow Stinger turned mid-flight to unleash a blast of sticky fire, which missed the dragon and hit the side of a building.

Smoke billowed up as flame crashed against steel, melting the metal and glass down the beams. Exposed wires sizzled and popped.

Ally gave chase as Sax steered his dragon down through the streets, scaring taxi and delivery dragons out of the way, and nearly knocking a bus off its dragon's back. Then it crashed straight through an open market on a high veranda of one of the buildings. Ally flew over it, avoiding the wreckage that Sax left in his wake.

"How come the police aren't showing up?" Abel wondered. "They're destroying property and maybe injuring people all over the city."

"The kin pay them to look the other way," Roa explained. "They won't show up unless the battle gets out of hand."

Just then, the Widow Maker used its wing to smash the glass off a building, creating a cloud of sharp shards that Ally had to fly through. All that glass fell toward the plaza below, where people ran for cover.

"This isn't out of hand?" Abel gawked at the destruction. He hoped the battle would end soon so that no innocent people got hurt. He didn't even care who won!

. . . Until he remembered that if it was the Red Talons, he'd have to fly in one of these battles next week. *"Come on, Ally,"* he whispered.

"I'm trying!" his teacher yelled back. He kept forgetting she could hear him.

Abel lost track of the Widow Maker when it suddenly dropped down from the clouds between two skyscrapers.

"Watch out!" Jusif warned. "He's right behind you!"

"I know." Ally flapped her dragon directly in front of Sax. Even without binoculars, Abel could see bursts of red gems shimmering in the lights of the city. They engulfed Ally and her dragon.

"Ally!" Roa yelled. The Red Talons ground crew looked over and laughed. It was a direct hit.

Abel stared through the binoculars as the Yellow Stinger dropped, plummeting between two buildings. She cried out as she fell, and Abel felt like he was falling with them, his heart sinking for the dragon and Ally. And for himself. A losing battle meant bad things for him.

But the Yellow Stinger caught herself just before hitting the pavement. She whirled and flapped clumsily to stay in the air. She was injured, but Ally looked like she was still okay and still in control of her dragon. The injured wings made her wobble and veer to the side, flying even slower than a toothless preschool bus, but she *was* flying.

"At this rate, you'll never make it back here for repairs," Olus said.

"I'm not coming in for repairs," Ally told them.

"Your dragon's hurt," Roa said.

"Which is my cover," Ally replied. Then, making it look like she was turning sideways because of her dragon's injuries, she instead pointed the dragon's nose straight for the school she'd flown over at the start of the battle. It was the place where she'd *actually* seen the hoard. While the Red Talons were looking in the wrong spot, she hit a button, revealing two huge jets on the back of her dragon's arms. She fired them, and the dragon no longer had to flap, only aim. She was rocket-powered!

A race, a heist, and a duel, Abel reminded himself, but realized those things didn't happen in order. They happened at the same time!

The dragon rocketed across the city, sweeping in low over the school and then up again. Ally turned back for the Glass Flats at wing-blurring speed.

"Sax, you idiot! It was a trick!" one of the Red Talons ground crew yelled.

Abel saw the gleam of the large golden token clutched in the yellow dragon's claws as it blasted over the city. The jewels caught the neon lights and sparkled as it flew.

Sax whirled to try to catch the jet-propelled dragon.

"Never bet against smarts and invention, kids," Olus told them. "Thunder Wings smarts beat Red Talons brawn any day."

"We haven't won yet," Abel said. The Widow Maker flew faster than he'd ever seen a dragon fly, trying to cut off Ally's approach to their spray-painted circle.

The blue flame jets on the yellow dragon's back sputtered out, and Ally slowed. Yellow Stingers were designed for bursts of speed, not long flights. Now the dragon had to flap under its own power the rest of the way.

As it got closer, Abel lowered the binoculars and watched with his bare eyes. He could see the effort it took the dragon to fly. Ally's move might've been a trick, but the injuries were real. Instructor Ally had purposefully let her dragon get hurt to win the kin battle.

The thought made Abel's stomach turn. When he looked at Roa, his best friend was chewing on their lip, distraught. They started to arrange bandages and ointments for when the dragon landed.

"She's not gonna make it . . ." Jusif warned. The Widow Maker was closing the distance fast, mouth opening to let loose another jet of razor-sharp shards of stone.

"*We're* not gonna make it!" Abel yelled, realizing that they were in a perfectly straight line with the attacking dragon. If its breath weapon missed Ally, it would hit the ground crew. In fact, it looked like the dragon was *aiming* for the ground crew!

They scattered, diving in every direction as the blast came in, shredding their equipment and the medical supplies.

"AHHHH!" Jusif screamed. From the way he writhed on the ground with his hands over his head, Abel was sure he'd be hit. "My hair!" He moved his hands to show a huge streak where one of the shards had shaved a line of hair away. "I'll tear your hearts out!" he yelled at the cackling Red Talons ground crew, charging at them as he pulled out a switchblade.

"Easy, boy!" Olus held him back. "No ground crew violence in a kin battle! Save it for a street fight!"

One of the Red Talons stuck out his tongue at Jusif, who was near tears with rage.

"Get off me!" Roa shouted at Topher. The boy had tackled them out of harm's way.

"You're welcome," Topher grumbled, helping Roa up.

The attack on the landing zone forced Ally to swerve off course, and now the Yellow Stinger and the Widow Maker circled each other overhead. Ally was trying to get over the spray-painted Thunder Wings symbol so she could drop the token and win. The Widow Maker blocked her every move. She feinted left and swung right, but the Widow Maker was there with a roar. She dove low and rolled, and there it was again with slashing claws. Ally's dragon was tiring, dripping gleaming drops of sizzling dragon's blood to the ground.

The Widow Maker lunged for a final assault. Ally's dragon darted forward, both of them roaring so loudly the glass vibrated beneath Abel's feet. He slammed his eyes shut, unable to watch the huge beasts clash.

His eyes were still closed when the cheering from his side erupted and the Red Talons cursed and bellowed.

"We won, Stable Abel!" Jusif yelled. "Open your eyes!" Abel peeked out to see Ally sitting atop her dragon in the Thunder Wings' circle, arms raised in victory. Bloody Zoonia clutched the token hoard greedily and panted with heavy-lidded eyes. Roa raced over to help the injured dragon. Ally dismounted and came to Abel.

"Nice job tonight," she said. "You used your brain and helped me trick the Red Talons. That kind of thinking will serve you well."

"What about your dragon?" he asked.

"Dragons are tough," she said. "She'll heal. What did you learn tonight, Abel?"

Abel thought about it for a moment; he looked at the Red Talons yelling at each other, and at Olus carrying a huge muzzle toward the Widow Maker, now the Thunder Wings' Widow Maker. He looked at the wounded Yellow Stinger, and at Jusif's wounded hair, and at Topher cleaning up the mess of dented and broken equipment. He looked back at his teacher, whose shoulder was bleeding.

"No one really wins a kin battle?" he suggested.

His teacher let out a sad smile, but she didn't tell him he was wrong.

16

THERE WAS BAD NEWS WAITING for Abel when he got home, though it looked exactly like his sister.

"Lina!" He ran to her when he saw her on the couch, almost knocking her over with his hug.

"Sweet sulfur skies, you stink!" She shoved him off and squeezed her nose dramatically.

"You're okay!" he cheered. Which, of course, she knew already. He glanced at his parents, both sitting on chairs opposite Lina. They looked stricken, and not by his smell. "What happened?" he asked.

Sax hadn't been happy to lose to the Thunder Wings. Maybe he took it out on Abel's family. But they'd won the battle and the Red Talons had to forgive Lina. That was the bet! Abel wanted to tell her about it, how he'd helped save her.

"Did the Red Talons go away?" he asked. "Did you go to the Half-Wing? They said by tomorrow! Are you really a—"

"Calm down, Abel," his father said.

"Why don't you shower?" his mother suggested. "After that, you can tell us all about your day with your teacher."

"But I—"

"Shower. Now." His mother was not negotiating.

• • •

By the time he was out and dressed again, Lina had gone to her bedroom. It was late, but Abel was still upset she didn't wait for him. There was so much he wanted to talk about.

"She's been awake for days, Abel," his father said. "Cut her some slack."

"But I—" He was about to say, *I've been training the dragon* she *stole and I just helped win a kin battle that saved our whole family from the Red Talons*, but he stopped himself. Instead, he said, "I wanted to see her. What happened?"

"You don't need to worry about it," his father told him. "It's taken care of."

"It is? How?"

"Don't worry about it," his dad repeated. Like Abel could stop worrying about the kinners or the secret police or their debts just because his father told him to. "How was your day? Did you eat any dinner?"

Abel crossed his arms. "Don't worry about it," he snapped. He turned to go back to his room. His stomach grumbled, but he'd already made his dramatic exit and couldn't go back to the kitchen now.

He sat on his bed and drummed his fingers on his knees, then stood up and did some stretches. He paced in circles. He thought about going down the hall and waking Lina up, demanding she tell him about being a dragon thief, about the Red Talons, and what he was supposed to do now that Karak had chosen him.

Instead, he checked his email. There was one from Ally, with a link to homework reading. *Really?* he thought. *Even after today, I have weekend reading?*

Homework was like feeding a dragon. Just as soon as you'd

washed the smell of burned goat from your clothes, it was time for the next one. It never ended.

When he opened the document, it was just page after page of letters and numbers and symbols that didn't look like anything. After staring at it for a full minute, a little box popped up asking him to enter a password.

"It's encrypted," he told himself, which was a way for documents to be scrambled so no one could read them unless they had the password. The only problem was, he didn't have it, and he couldn't remember his teacher telling him one. Had he tuned out and missed it, or was this another test, like making him put on Karak's saddle without telling him how?

He was about to text Roa to ask for help when he realized— if his teacher was sending him encrypted homework, it was because she didn't want anyone else knowing what it said. Did that mean someone else was *already* reading his emails somehow?

The Thunder Wings were the only kin technologically advanced enough to pull that off. Abel didn't think they would monitor the emails that a seventh grader got from their own kinner . . . but the Dragon's Eye definitely would.

If the Dragon's Eye were still looking for Lina, they were probably reading the whole family's emails *and* texts. He didn't want to drag Roa into that. His best friend could do real jail time if they got caught. Then again, he could too.

But if the Dragon's Eye were watching his email, they were probably watching his apartment . . . which meant they'd already know Lina was here.

So why weren't they bursting in to arrest her right now?

Abel listened for a moment, as if just by thinking about getting arrested, he'd summoned the tactical squad to bust down the door and take his whole family away. But all he heard was some audiobook about "finding the dragon within the self" that his dad was listening to in the kitchen. There were screeches and roars from the air traffic outside, shouts from pilot to pilot as passenger dragons and commercial dragons and private dragons weaved around each other in the bustling city sprawl. But no police raids. Not yet.

Abel looked at his blinking cursor in the password box.

Focus, he told himself. *Remember everything Instructor Ally said.*

In school, she was a tough teacher, but she was fair, and she'd never tried to trick her students or catch them out for no reason. When she presented a problem in class, there was always a solution. "If you use the brains you haven't fried on games."

This was the same. She wanted him to use his brain, just like he had in the kin battle. What did he know that could be a password? He entered a try:

THUNDER WING

The screen flashed:

INCORRECT PASSWORD.

1st Attempt of 3.

"What happens after three?" he muttered.

He stared at the cursor and his brain went blank. He had

less than zero ideas. Negative ideas. He felt like he was getting dumber just sitting there trying to think of something smart. He pounded the keys, which he regretted the moment after he'd done it.

;HGPWEUR!HFBDL!

The screen flashed:

INCORRECT PASSWORD.

2nd Attempt of 3.

He dropped his head into his hands. Percy, perched on the end of the bed, looked up at him, sniffed his foot, then curled his scaly body around himself again, cooing.

How was he supposed to do this? He couldn't do the homework if he couldn't even open it. And if he didn't do the homework, would Ally fail him? Abel wasn't being graded, so what did failing even mean? He thought about how willing she'd been to let her dragon get hurt in order to win the battle. A dragon was worth a lot more to the Thunder Wings than he was. They said Abel owed them for making the Red Talons back off Lina. If he failed them, would they feed him and Roa to their dragons?

And then what would happen to his parents? To Lina? Would the Red Talons come back to finish them off? Would Silas get kicked out of the Academy for having siblings involved in illegal kin activity? Would they have to hire a lawyer they couldn't afford and make Dad go back to work in the farming towers, breathing in the same fumes that got him sick in the first place? Would they all end up in Windlee Prison? Or perhaps exiled or buried in an unmarked hole in the Glass Flats?

Those dreadful futures shot out in front of him like fire from Karak's mouth. Abel couldn't stop himself from imagining all of them in vivid detail. It was like the ideas had talons gripped on to his brain.

The school counselor he'd seen while his father was sick told him this was called "catastrophizing." His mind jumped to the worst possible outcome and then fixated on it. He did it all the time, but it was never helpful. And the things he came up with were rarely true. The counselor had taught him strategies for breaking the catastrophizing loops. Take deep breaths. Observe the thoughts but let them pass like traffic flying by outside the window. Try to focus on a different, positive outcome—which was just as made up as the bad ones anyway. "If you can imagine storms, you can imagine rainbows," the counselor had advised. "Inhale. Count to four. Exhale. Imagine the rainbow. What is your rainbow?"

Sometimes Abel imagined Dr. Drago and what he would do. Drago wouldn't freak out. He wouldn't catastrophize. What would Dr. Drago do? He'd crack the password.

WW3D. WW3D.

Focusing on the simple phrase over and over helped. It was all about trying to break the loop of negative thoughts.

The loop.

His mind snagged on that word.

Everything means something, Ally had said during training, when she was quizzing them on the OODA loop. *Observe. Orient. Decide. Act.*

She'd also said it when he and Roa repeated WW3D to each other.

Everything means something.

He took a deep breath and then typed in the password box:

OODA WW3D

Suddenly, the text on the screen sorted itself, transforming from total gibberish into actual words and illustrations.

He whooped and pumped his fists. VICTORY!

And then he deflated again.

"Oh right," he grumbled, looking at the dense essay about dragon biology in front of him. "It's homework."

• • •

Hours later, Abel startled awake. A string of drool connected his face and his screen, where he'd been reading about the temperature differences in the breath weapons of different combat dragons. Somewhere along the way, he'd realized this was a stolen dragon cadet textbook, not meant to be read by anyone outside the Academy.

That didn't make it any more exciting. He'd read three different theories on hoarding behavior among medium-wing Reaper-class dragons and their implications for "field deployment," which he didn't really understand. Then, all of a sudden, he was up to his eyeballs in a chapter about secretions from a dragon's oral glands, producing "breath-propelled events," which he guessed was just the most boring way of saying "weapons."

He didn't see how knowing any of this would make him better in a kin battle on Karak's back.

He also didn't see how he'd ever read it all tonight. The clock said it was 1:02 a.m. The billboard outside flashed its bright neon against his window. He peered at the city sky, soothed by the blinking lights and flashing signs and endless bustle in skyscraper after skyscraper. Abel loved the city. It was like a dragon all its own. Everyone in it was just another scale—unique, connected, and tougher than they looked. He hoped he was tougher than he looked. He'd need to be if he was going to get his family out of the trouble they were in.

He heard a sound outside his door. At first he thought it was Percy scratching to be let in, but (a) pangolins didn't scratch gently, and (b) Percy was already asleep at his feet. It sounded like his sister talking.

Abel slipped out of bed, padded across the room, and peeked into the hall. He was just in time to see his mother open the apartment door in her bathrobe as his father gave Lina a long, tearful hug. Lina was dressed in an orange-red-and-blue zippered jumpsuit, with intricate stitching and complicated zippers. It was one of her favorite outfits. Where was she going dressed like that at 1:02 in the morning? And why were Mom and Dad letting her?

"You promise me she'll be taken care of," Mom said to a figure standing in the open door. "Promise me she can count on you."

"Of course," the figure answered. Abel's heart jumped as his brother, Silas, stepped into the apparent in his long cadet's overcoat. He gave their mom a hug. "This really is for the best. As long as she cooperates."

142

"Of course I'll cooperate," Lina said. "As long as your fascist bosses keep their end of the bargain."

"They are not fascists," Silas grunted. "And it's dangerous to talk that way."

"I'd rather say dangerous things than let them turn me into a fool," Lina snapped at him.

"It's not foolish to obey the law," Silas said.

"Whose law?" Lina answered.

"There's only one law, and it's going to save your—" Silas started to respond.

"Enough!" their father interrupted. "You're siblings. You have to take care of each other. No matter *what*. Family is the most important thing."

"That's why I'm doing this, Dad," Lina said. "For our family."

"Me too." Silas looked at his watch—a green-and-silver device with a black touchscreen that was way nicer than anything their household owned. He tapped his foot impatiently, then tapped the watch screen a few times. "Time to go."

Lina nodded and hugged their mom. "You'll explain to Abel?"

"We'll tell him you're doing the right the thing," his mother said.

"Or you could tell him the truth," Lina said sadly. "He can handle more than you think."

"He's got enough going on," Mom said. "With school closed and his work for his teacher. We'll decide what your little brother can handle."

"You trust his teacher?" Lina asked.

"Of course we do," his father said.

"Okay . . ." Lina said doubtfully. Did she know Ally was a Thunder Wing?

"Better not to tell him about any of this," Silas said. "What he doesn't know can't hurt him."

Abel wanted to rush out of the room and demand they explain what was going on, but he knew they wouldn't tell him.

Anyway, it was too late. Silas took Lina by the arm, and they left. Abel watched as his mother locked the door, then rested her head on the doorframe and began to cry. His father held her, whispering things Abel couldn't hear.

No one should have to watch their parents cry, Abel thought. He didn't like it.

Why had Lina come home when she was on the run from the law and the kins? Why was she going off with Silas in the middle of the night? And *what* didn't they want Abel to know?

"Only one way to find out," Abel whispered to himself. He watched his parents trudge down the hall to their bedroom and close the door.

He didn't wait long. Carrying his shoes in his hands, he snuck out of the apartment, after his brother and sister. On his way out, he heard his parents whispering in their room. They'd be sound asleep soon.

At least, he hoped they would. If he got caught sneaking out, he wouldn't need to worry about the Red Talons, or the Thunder Wings, or the Dragon's Eye . . . his parents would kill him first!

17

ABEL HAD NEVER BEEN OUTSIDE this late before. The night streets belonged to the neon signs and the blinking billboards and the holographic advertisements that flickered and wavered in the drizzle of spring rain. Puddles on the concrete reflected the shimmering skyscrapers upside down, like there was an endless city below the streets, glimpsed only through rippling holes in the sidewalk.

Abel stared down at the puddle he'd just stepped in, soaking his untied sneakers. The neon curlicues from the noodle shop sign across the street splattered into pink static. Behind his reflection, he saw the shadow of a long-wing freight dragon glide over the tops of the buildings, hauling deliveries on its lonely route. He thought about Ally's injured dragon and all the ways humans used these mighty creatures.

Maybe, he thought, *it isn't really for their own good at all. Maybe people keep telling these old stories about dragons so that nothing has to change.*

He looked up from his feet just in time to see Silas and Lina turn the corner toward a public landing zone. He pulled his hoodie up over his head and tried to keep to the shadows against the buildings as he followed.

"It's not too late for you," Lina was telling Silas as he hauled her by the arm. "You can still be a good person."

"I *am* a good person, Li," Silas said back to her. "Just because I don't share your 'moral code' doesn't mean I don't have one."

"You have whatever moral code they've told you to have at the Academy," she said.

"That's not fair," Silas replied. "I believe in something more than——"

Abel lost their conversation as they turned again, toward a wider street. Seventeenth Avenue, he thought. Or was it Eighteenth? He was all turned around, even though this was his neighborhood. At night, nothing looked quite the same.

The holographic sign outside the landing zone advertised the cost of parking a private dragon there, but the machine that gave out tickets and opened the gate was wrapped in yellow caution tape. The zone was closed. Silas walked past it without looking.

"I'm trying to *protect* you," Lina told Silas.

"Worry about yourself," Silas said. "Tell the whole truth and it'll go a lot easier for you. And for Mom and Dad."

"Let me go," Lina said. "Tell them I escaped. The Dragon's Eye can't punish you for being overpowered by your . . . *stronger* sister."

Abel laughed at that one. When Silas was fourteen and Lina was eleven, he took one of her books and ripped it. They got into a fight, and she didn't just beat Silas; she *dominated* him. He had to scream for mercy and for Mom, the two things no prideful boy like Silas ever wanted to do. He'd never recovered. Abel, on the other hand, had never been in a fight in his life.

"You are *not* stronger than me," Silas grumbled. "And

anyway, the Dragon's Eye won't punish me. You don't know what you're talking about."

"I know more than you think," Lina replied.

Abel stepped in a puddle that was deeper than it looked, and almost tripped over on a broken piece of sidewalk. The noise made his siblings turn around, and he had to press himself behind the nearest object, a stinking trash can in front of a cheap sandwich shop. Silas scanned the sidewalk as Abel held his breath. Lina, however, looked totally relaxed.

Well, *that* made no sense. Silas was arresting *her*, probably turning her over to the Dragon's Eye. But she didn't seem worried at all, while Silas looked terrified. He pulled Lina on. They went around another corner, down one of the unnamed streets that zigzagged and crisscrossed the neighborhood. They were hidden from above by low concrete slabs so that surveyor dragons didn't even know these covered alleys existed. It made Abel think of the old fable that little kids learn, about how dragons fight in the skies, but flowers still grow on the ground.

A fortune-teller's storefront glimmered in neon green on the corner. Next door was a bright hologram of children playing with tiny newborn drakes and dragonets, advertising a day care that probably had one sickly, retired NERD for the kids to play with.

Just as Abel moved to follow his brother and sister, a voice called to him from an open storefront across the street. "Hey, kiddo, what are you doing out here past your bedtime?"

He looked up, shielding his eyes from the light that spilled out of Duvrell's Twenty-Four-Hour Laundromat-Casino. A hostess in a long red dress made to look like dragon scales leaned on the store's doorframe, holding a tattered paperback book. There were no customers inside, so she was probably bored.

"You don't know my bedtime," he called back to her. Abel recognized the hostess from the neighborhood. She was nice, always leaving scraps of her breakfast for the stray street pangolins, drakes, and wyrmlings that wandered around in the morning, scrounging for food.

She laughed as Abel glanced toward the alley where Silas and Lina had gone. He'd lost them.

"If it's your brother you're after, I can just tell you where he's headed," the hostess said. "Save you some skulking in shadows. Come over here. No sense shouting private business. The streets have ears as well as eyes, you know."

Abel hesitated. Even in normal times, he wasn't supposed to talk to any of the hostesses at the little casinos around the neighborhood. They all worked for the Red Talons kin. But he was already breaking every rule he'd ever known, so what was one more?

He crossed the street.

"You're Abel, right?" the hostess asked. She was very tall and had to bend down to talk to him. She had a tattoo of the Red Talons kin on the side of her neck, and her perfume smelled sweet, like frosted cake. Her makeup was flecked with glitter that caught the neon lights around her and sparkled in every color of the rainbow. Her eyes were brilliant purple, which Abel knew had to be from contact lenses because *no one's* eyes were purple. "I'm Shivonne," she told him.

"A pleasure to meet you," he replied, remembering his

manners, even though it was after one in the morning and she was a hostess at a laundromat-casino. *Good manners are like black T-shirts*, his father always said. *Always in style*. "How do you know who I am?"

"I've worked at this laundry longer than you've been alive," she told him. "From this very door, I've watched all you kids grow up." She shook her head sadly. "And grow apart. I knew Lina and Silas would collide one of these days, from the first time I saw her painting graffiti and him tattling on her."

"How do you know where they're going?" Abel asked. He didn't have time to waste with a trip down memory's winding alleyways.

She pursed her lips and whispered in Abel's ear. "It's my job to know."

"But I thought you were—"

She cut him off with a gentle clucking sound. "I am many things to many people. But to this street, I am a pair of eyes that see everything, ears that hear everything, and lips that stay tightly sealed." She winked at him as she pressed one of her long and colorful fingernails to her lips. Her bracelets slipped down, and Abel saw a small tattoo of another kin's symbol on her wrist: the laughing dragon of the Wind Breakers kin. She pulled the bracelets back into place to cover it and winked at him.

"Hey, Shiv!" another voice from within the laundromat shouted. "Stop talking to that street kid and help me move this thing! Grackle wants it on the other side of the store."

Abel's stomach wrapped around his heart at the mention of Grackle. He looked around for the tuft of blue hair, but Shivonne put her a hand on his shoulder. "Relax, he's not here," she said. "He and Sax went off to harass some other innocent families in the middle of the night. Sax was in a *mood*. I hear he lost a valuable dragon in a battle tonight . . . but you're too young to know anything about that, right?"

Did she just wink at him again? Did she know?

"Anyway," Shivonne continued. "Your brother chose this moment to leave while they're gone. In spite of what your sister thinks, Silas is nobody's fool."

Just then, from an alley down the street, a silver-scaled wyvern stalked out. It looked up and down with gleaming golden eyes. The eyes narrowed in Abel's direction. Shivonne stepped slightly in front of him, obscuring the dragon's view.

The wyvern wore a harness with reins attached that led back to a rider's saddle just behind the base of its skull. The figure in the saddle was only a silhouette, backlit by neon lights, but Abel would've known him anywhere: Silas.

Behind him was a long hard-shelled pod with air holes drilled through it and heavy locks on the outside. A prisoner carrier, and Abel was pretty sure his sister was inside it. At the back of the wyvern, just in front of its tail, sat a rear-facing harness with a big mounted flamethrower. A second figure sat at it, scanning the opposite direction from the wyvern's eyes. Abel couldn't make that figure out, but he caught the gleam of their night vision goggles.

"That's a Dragon's Eye assault wyvern," he gasped.

The silver wyvern ran forward on its two legs and leapt into the air with a thrust. Its wings flapped and it rose over the fortune-teller's, flying straight through a huge hologram ad for the next Dragon Guard movie—*Drakonia and the Desert of Lies*—then out of sight.

"Your brother's not just a cadet at the Academy," Shivonne told Abel quietly. "He's also an agent of the Dragon's Eye. He's taking your sister to their headquarters for interrogation."

"No . . ." Abel said, shock hitting him like a blast of cold wind across his face. "He can't . . . He wouldn't . . ."

"If she cooperates with the Dragon's Eye and turns in other members of the Sky Knights, then the government can protect your family from the Red Talons. That's the deal they made."

"No." Abel shook his head. "I took care of it already. We *won*. They didn't have to do this."

"I heard Sax telling Grackle himself," she said. "They had to back off your family to avoid trouble with the Eye themselves. It's an uneasy truce between the law and the kin."

"Silas *wouldn't* do that . . ." Abel said. But even as he said it, he knew it was exactly the kind of thing Silas would do.

"He's trying to protect you and your parents. So is Lina." She squeezed Abel's shoulder. "If you're still set on following them, I wouldn't recommend it. Drakopolis at night is no place for children."

Abel looked up in the direction his brother had flown and then back in the direction of his apartment building. His sister was a criminal, and his brother was secret police. His parents had let his brother arrest his sister. He knew he should really just go back to bed, but he felt sick. His family was tearing itself apart. Someone had to stop it, and Abel figured he was the only one who could.

Well, Abel and his Sunrise Reaper.

"I can handle it," he said, straightening his back and putting his hood up again. "Any chance I could borrow some money for a taxi? I've got a dragon waiting for me across town."

The hostess sighed and glanced over her shoulder. She slipped a small bedazzled phone out of a hidden pocket in her dress and tapped a few buttons. Abel's phone buzzed in his pocket. She'd summoned a ride for him.

"Thanks," he said. "I'll pay you back."

"No need," she told him. "Your dad always smiles at me when he does the laundry, and your sister gives me the romance novels I like for free. Keep them all safe, and we'll call it even. But can I give you one piece of advice?"

"Yeah?" Abel waited.

"The city will teach you hard lessons. Don't let them make less of you."

Abel didn't know what that meant, but he reassured her anyway. "I won't. I promise."

Moments later, a short-winged Green Whiffler landed in front of him, and he clambered into the passenger harness. "Where to?" the driver asked. Abel gave him the address.

"That's a bad part of town," the driver said. "Nothing but warehouses and Thunder Wings goons. What's a kid like you doing there at an hour like this?"

"Not answering questions, for one," Shivonne called up to the driver. "Leave the kid be." She tapped her phone again, and the pilot's screen pinged. Shivonne had given him a big tip.

"Thank you!" Abel called as the dragon ran past her, picking up speed for takeoff.

As they launched into the night air, Abel considered how

strange it was that someone he'd always learned to be afraid of could be so generous and open, while the people he'd always trusted were hoarding secrets like a dragon hoards treasure.

People are complicated, he thought. And he realized as he flew over the city's late-night gleam and glare that he was becoming complicated too.

He liked the feeling.

WHEN HE GOT TO THE old can factory across town, the taxi couldn't drop him off fast enough. Which was good, because Abel was in a hurry.

They say no plan made after midnight can ever come to good, but Abel had never thought of a plan after midnight before. He hoped he'd have what they called beginner's luck.

He also had no idea who *they* were but would prefer to stay out of *their* sayings altogether. No good ever came from being the main character in a saying.

Abel looked around for Jusif and the other Thunder Wings kinners, but they were all in the alley, still loudly celebrating the kin battle victory. Abel used his keycard to slip inside the building, and he navigated along the catwalks with the light from his phone. He didn't risk turning the lights on.

Karak was wide-awake, sitting on his hoard of cans. The dragon used one long claw to bowl a can into a huge pyramid of them across the factory floor.

Karak missed the shot just as Abel came in. He roared in frustration before he noticed Abel standing on the catwalk. The dragon's nose turned from deep black to a light gray. Abel wondered if that was how Sunrise Reapers blushed.

"It's okay," he told the dragon, not sure how much he understood. "I get bored and distracted sometimes too."

The dragon turned all black again, swinging his head around so he was right in front of Abel.

"You want to take a little trip through the city?" he asked. Before the sentence was even out of his mouth, Karak had extended his neck for Abel to climb aboard.

Abel put the saddle on in the dark, glad for all the practice Ally had made him do. He paused for just a moment to wonder if it was really wise to go after a fully armed Dragon's Eye wyvern in the dead of night when no one except a hostess at a laundromat-casino knew where he was.

Then again, no one had ever accused Abel of being wise.

He spurred Karak to fly. The dragon took a running start and leapt into the air, streaking across the factory toward the giant loading dock doors and bursting out into the night.

They flew fast and low over the district of warehouses, weaving through the shadows of dilapidated billboards and half-ruined skyscrapers, slicing through holographic ads for movies and medicines and megastores that sold everything from movies to medicines.

They weaved between rusted cranes, past buildings that never finished going up and buildings that never finished coming down. They flapped past a skyscraper that was missing an entire wall, and Abel saw that hundreds of people had rigged up little shacks and houses inside it, using all kinds of scraps and discarded pieces of garbage. Laundry hung on lines where someone had once planned to put fancy offices.

Folks had constructed rickety bridges between the high floors of some of these ruined skyscrapers, connecting one to the other. It was like the skybridge in the fancier parts of the city, but made of the chains and ropes that the fancier parts of the city threw away. It was a whole other city within the city Abel knew, off all the official maps.

Abel took note of the graffiti on some of the bridges and a few of the collapsing walls. There were the usual nicknames of the artists, and bits of slang he didn't know, and curse words he wasn't supposed to know. But there were also stencils of the laughing dragon of the Wind Breakers kin, who didn't, as far as Abel knew, control any territory. These buildings were lawless places, beyond not only the rule of Dragon's Eye and the City Council, but even the other kins.

The city he'd lived in his whole life was a lot like the people he'd known his whole life: filled with secrets and surprises he'd never dreamed of, secrets that were scary but also exciting.

They flew on in the dark, unseen by the patrols riding long-wings high above, or the short-wing officers monitoring the streets below. The middle heights of the city belonged to the medium-wing dragons—like the wyverns and the reapers—and to the kinners who flew them.

They also belonged to the Dragon's Eye, who went wherever they pleased. The secret police had informants in every shadow and knew far more than even the City Council, who they worked for. It was hard to believe his brother was one of them.

Abel caught a glimpse of Silas's silver wyvern flapping across the colorful twirling laser lights of the Raptura District, where all the theaters and nightclubs and dance halls were. He leaned and turned Karak in that direction, speeding up.

He could see the Dragon's Eye headquarters looming up in Center City. It was a huge corkscrew-shaped building, made entirely out of dragon glass. Depending on the time of day and the way the light hit, it glowed orange and red and green and blue. Even at night, it caught the lights of the city. Dragons flew in and out of it at all hours. The Dragon's Eye never slept; it was always open, always watching. The thought made him shiver.

Abel had to intercept his brother's wyvern before it got to headquarters, or he might never see his sister again. The bright pink and green lights of the Dancing Dragon Circus Show bounced off the wyvern's silver scales. He turned Karak wide. If he came up straight behind the wyvern, the tail gunner with the night vision goggles and the flamethrower would see him. He had to sweep in from the side and—

And what? he asked himself.

He hadn't thought this through very well. He didn't want to hurt anyone, not Silas or Lina or the wyvern or the tail gunner. But he needed to get them to the ground so he could at least talk to Silas. *How do you force a wyvern to the ground without hurting anyone?*

And then he knew. It's what he did with Silas all the time. He could pick a fight without planning to win it.

Abel leaned low into Karak's back so that they wouldn't be able to see him clearly, and poured on the speed. Karak flapped madly—the dragon seemed to be enjoying it. They raced toward the wyvern, Abel's hair fluttering and his eyes stinging. He'd have to get a pair of aviator glasses, like literally every other dragon rider had.

At the edge of the Raptura District, they blasted through a huge hologram ad for Hot Pepper N' Cocoa Covered Wyvern Wafers, swooping his dragon through the chocolates just as they snapped apart. If anyone was looking up from their partying, all they would've noticed was one big dark crumb slightly larger than the others breaking free from the ad and disappearing with a glimmer of starlight.

Abel pulled back on Karak's spine to get him flying almost straight up. He aimed for the space in the sky between two bright circus lights, so that Karak's body would be invisible in the dark. Then he got right above his brother's wyvern and leaned forward.

Karak hesitated.

"Come on, buddy, this is it," he pleaded. "Dive!"

Karak tucked his wings. For a moment, all was still and Abel felt weightless. Then came the fall.

As Karak's nose pointed down between the buildings, Abel's legs flew up behind him and his whole body floated upward. Only his hands clutching a knob on the dragon's spine kept him from spinning off into the dark sky. The lights of the city filled his eyes, looming huge. Abel had trouble focusing on the silver glint of the wyvern in between all the bright colors and flashing lasers, but Karak knew what to do. He buzzed right past the silver wyvern, just barely clipping its wings and letting out a blood-boiling roar as he did it.

"AHHHHHH!" Abel didn't even know he was screaming until they were already past the wyvern, nearly down at ground level. Then, suddenly, they were looping up again. Karak's claws sparked off the sidewalk pavement, sending the groundwyrms that pulled food carts and pedicabs along the plaza scrambling out of the way.

Karak flew low, and Abel did his best to steer through the

busy lanes. He dared a glance over his shoulder to make sure that Silas was following him. Turning like that made him dizzy, though, and now he understood why dragon pilots had rearview mirrors set into their goggles. Looking backward while flying at dragon-chase speeds was a recipe for high-velocity vomit.

Abel kept his eyes forward and took deep breaths through his nose, just like he did when the school bus hit bumpy wind.

In his hands, he felt Karak's bones getting hotter, and the seams between his deep black scales glowed orange. The dragon began to turn toward the wyvern.

"No, no, no, no, no, no, no," Abel pleaded, trying to pull Karak's reins so he straightened out again. "No fire . . . no killing . . . just . . . no!"

The dragon twisted his head around and glared at Abel, still flying forward at full speed. Abel could see the glow inside his mouth. He feared for a second his new partner might incinerate him, except he was on the dragon's own back. He wasn't sure if dragons could set themselves on fire or not, but he didn't imagine this one would enjoy finding out.

Karak snorted smoke and sparks and straightened his neck again, stretching his body into a sleek line and putting on more speed. The wyvern with the flamethrower was more maneuverable than the reaper, just like in DrakoTek, but it was much slower on straightaways. Abel had to slow Karak down to keep them close. He pressed himself down against Karak's back as flat as he could and hoped Silas hadn't recognized him.

The sudden jet of green poison that blasted just over his head made it pretty clear he hadn't. Or it meant that Silas was trying to kill his own little brother, which was unlikely . . . but not impossible.

Abel leaned sideways to avoid the next blast of the wyvern's breath weapon. Karak rolled in a corkscrew, spinning upside down and around and around. Abel held on. His head barely missed the pavement as they swirled, and his knuckles turned white gripping the saddle. He'd forgotten to clip in to his safety harness! Only the force of the spin kept him from falling off. Karak flew straight toward the huge stone-and-glass entrance to a fancy restaurant with its own landing platform halfway up the building.

"AHH!" Abel screamed, and pulled back on the reins. An instant before they would have crashed into the restaurant, Karak turned straight up the front of the sleek skyscraper, the glittering reflection of his belly just an arm's length away.

They lost some speed on the turn. In the reflection off the building, Abel saw the silver wyvern right behind them, almost close enough to bite Karak's tail. Another poison-green glow formed in its mouth.

From what he'd learned in the homework Ally had given him, a wyvern's poison breath was harmless to other dragons but could paralyze a full-grown man for three days. And that was *if* the wyvern chose not to eat him immediately, or in slow and painful pieces. An orb of swirling green poison was building up pressure in its throat. Abel might've stood a chance if he'd had a protective suit, but all he had was a hoodie and hope.

He risked looking back over his shoulder again. This time, he needed Silas to see his face. They were flying straight up a build-ing, so looking back really meant looking straight down. If it had made him a little dizzy when they were flying horizontally, vertically it made him completely ill. The people outside the restaurants and theaters of the plaza were the size of bugs. The lights from of the city swirled and danced and spun. If he fell, it looked like he might fall forever and never actually hit the ground.

Not if *I fall*, his spinning mind catastrophized, *but* when.

That was, of course, the moment his hands slipped.

Abel fell straight for the gaping maw of the wyvern and his brother's startled face.

19

ABEL TUMBLED OUT OF THE saddle, lamenting his open safety harness clip. He rolled backward, head over heels, down the sparkling spine of his dragon.

As he fell, Karak shrieked. The wyvern let out its blast of poison in one long stream, straight at the spot where Abel had been a moment before. Had he not fallen, he'd have taken the full brunt over his entire body.

Instead, he rocketed below the poison and through the air, right past his brother.

"Abel!" he heard Silas shout over the roar of the wind in his ears. The next thing he knew, both his reaper and Silas's wyvern had turned. They snapped at each other, chasing him down, each trying to catch him and to stop the other one from catching him.

They're both trying to save me, he thought. *And neither one is going to succeed.*

"Karak, break!" he shouted at the top of his lungs. Karak, to his great surprise, obeyed. His dragon broke away, letting the silver wyvern snatch Abel from the air with one huge foot. It turned and billowed up, above the lights and the blare of the city, to the top of the skyscraper he'd just been plummeting down the face of. It dropped him roughly down on the flat roof.

Karak landed right in front of him and lowered his head at the wyvern, jaws open and flame brewing, daring it to make one wrong move. The wyvern readied more poison breath. Abel stood on shaking legs, right between the two dragons. He raised his arms to each of them.

"Please, noble dragons. Both of you, stop!" Abel remembered his manners toward the proud dragons, but he also remembered his brother deserved no such politeness. So he added, "Silas, you dumpster-brained dingus, tell your dragon to stand down!"

"Easy, Wondla." Silas patted his wyvern. "Be easy, girl." Karak's flame cooled, and the wyvern gulped back her poison again.

Silas swung out of his harness and hopped down, just as the tail gunner leapt off from the back, their flamethrower still in their arms. They raised it straight at Abel.

"Hands behind your head!" they barked, voice distorted by their helmet. Their night vision goggles glowered at Abel like one single green eye.

Abel raised his hands over his head. He could insult his older brother all he wanted, but knew not to mouth off to the business end of a stranger's flamethrower.

"No, Kai, I got this," Silas told his partner. "It's okay. He's . . . my *little brother.*"

The way he said "little brother" made it sound like the worst insult imaginable, but Kai lowered the flamethrower and stepped away to lean on the side of the wyvern. He took his helmet off and revealed a lush crown of locks and dark skin dusted with fine gold powder. He rolled his eyes at Silas and at Abel. "Your family has issues, partner."

Silas got right in Abel's face, which made Karak growl and narrow his eyes. The wyvern hissed in return. "What under all the scorched skies are you doing?" Silas demanded. "And where did you get this dragon? And how did you learn to fly it? And . . . just . . ." He threw his hands in the air. "Just *what*?"

"You seem nonplussed." Abel grinned, trying to project a cool attitude. It would've been more effective if he didn't also feel like throwing up. His legs were still shaky, and there was a buzzing in his ears. He couldn't be 100 percent sure he hadn't peed himself during the fall. He did his best to keep himself together . . . and remember the huge black dragon that had his back.

WW3D, he psyched himself up in his head. *WW3D*.

"You're not the only one with secrets, Silas," he said. "Is it Cadet Silas or Agent Silas, by the way?"

Silas stiffened his lip. "Don't ask questions you don't want to know the answer to."

"Let Lina go," Abel said. "You can't take her in."

"She's a thief and criminal," Silas said. "She broke the law and put our family in danger. The best thing she can do now is tell the authorities the names of everyone with ties to her kin. *Maybe* the judge will go easy on her because she's under eighteen."

"The Sky Knights don't care that she's a teenager," Abel said. "If she snitches on her kin, they'll come after all of us. She won't be safe, even in Windlee Prison."

"The Dragon's Eye will protect her and all of you," Silas said.

"Yeah, they've done a great job so far," Abel answered. He thought about Topher, whose family the Dragon's Eye was also supposed to protect. "The Red Talons punched dad."

"You don't need to worry about those kinners anymore. They won't bother you. That's part of the arrangement."

"What arrangement? You mean the Dragon's Eye works with the Red Talons?"

"What did I say about not asking questions you don't want the answer to?"

"*Please* let Lina go," Abel tried with some emotion. He wasn't above begging, if he thought it would work. "You don't turn your family in. There has to be another way."

"You're lucky I don't arrest *you* right now," Silas said. "Go home, and maybe we can forget this. Just text me where you leave this stolen dragon. We can say Lina told us the location and return it to its owner. Your name doesn't need to come up, okay? You were never here."

"I didn't see anything," Kai added casually. "Definitely no junior high kids flying stolen Sunrise Reapers over an adults-only district so late at night it's almost morning. Nope, not a thing . . ."

"I'll count to five," Silas warned Abel.

"You can't order me around." Abel crossed his arms. "You're not Mom and Dad."

"I *can* order your around, Abel." Silas taped a pin on his flight jacket. A cyclops dragon wielding a sword, the emblem of the Dragon's Eye. "We're the law in this city, which means you do what I say, or else."

"You're a bully and traitor to our family," Abel grunted.

Silas shook his head. "Will you stop being so dramatic for one second? This was Lina's idea. She knew either the Red Talons would catch her or we would. She turned herself in to protect you and Mom and Dad from the kin. You think you're helping her, but you're not, okay? So go home and play with your cards and let the big kids handle this."

"*She* thought of this?" Abel looked up at the prisoner pod on the wyvern's back. He remembered how relaxed Lina looked when Silas took her out of the apartment. How she'd tried to warn Silas, like she knew something he didn't, even though she was the one being arrested.

When they were little, Silas could never beat Lina at DrakoTek. She always anticipated what card he was going to play next. One by one, she'd lay her cards to lure him right into a trap. Then she'd crush him just when he'd thought he'd won. Silas eventually refused to play her, because he hated losing so much. That was why she taught Abel how to play. He always lost to her too, but he still couldn't resist playing.

Abel remembered the noise that had summoned him from his room at 1:02 a.m., before his sister was led away. It was her voice that had woken him. *She* had made a noise loud enough to wake up him, even though he knew she could be as quiet as she wanted.

His heart raced.

His sister had woken up him on purpose . . . because she knew he couldn't resist. Right now both of her easily beaten brothers were together on a rooftop with not *one*, but *two* extremely valuable dragons.

This wasn't a card game, but Lina was playing just like she always had.

"She's set up an ambush," Abel gasped. "To steal back Karak—and your wyvern too!"

"What are you talking about?" Silas scoffed. "There's no ambu—"

"Sorry, bro," Lina interrupted him, no longer in the prisoner pod. In fact, she was now standing in front of Kai, aiming his own flamethrower back at him. "Nice to see you, Kai," she added. "Sorry it has to be like this, but of course, if you move, I'll barbecue you."

"Lina," Kai sighed.

"Lina!" Silas cried.

"Lina!" Abel shouted, just as a bright green Moss dragon scampered onto the roof from the side of the building. A matching pair of black Half-Wyverns swirled down through the dancing lights in the sky, circling just over them. Each had a rider and a gunner on board, the gunners each pointing big anti-dragon laser cannons down.

A blue-and-gray Steelwing Reaper landed opposite the Moss dragon. Its rider hopped off, raising his flight goggles as he did.

He was wearing a high-collared military officer's coat, but he'd traded out all the silver buttons for bright neon ones in red, orange, and blue. The Sky Knights emblem and snatches of graffiti were spray-painted all over the coat, along with patches and medals from victories his kin had claimed or from bands he just really liked. The other Sky Knights were dressed in the same colors with the same symbols all over them, in wildly different fabrics and styles. Abel figured kinship was half fashion, half criminal cruelty.

The rider in the captain's coat walked right up to Silas and Abel. He looked back and forth between them and their dragons.

"Well, well, well, Lina. These are fine specimens. You outdid yourself."

Lina tossed the flamethrower back to Kai, then undid a zipper on her own jumpsuit that opened a flap to reveal the infinity dragon emblem. "If you're feeling lucky, you can try to shoot that thing," she dared Kai, who grunted and set the flamethrower down. Lina turned to the Sky Knights leader. "Thank you, Captain Drey, for believing in me." She did a weird little hand gesture, touching her index fingers to the tip of the thumb on the opposite hand, making an infinity symbol. "I serve the eternal knight."

"Of course, the knight, yes," Captain Drey said back to her. He quickly made the same symbol with his hands, before dropping it just as quickly.

Lina didn't seem to mind; she had a fire in her eyes like Abel remembered her getting when she used to describe whatever banned book she was reading, earning eye rolls from her brothers and nervous laughter from their parents. Everyone had a few banned books in their homes, but nobody talked about them as much as Lina did.

The government was always banning and unbanning things, so it was hard to keep track. The City Council made random laws just so people ended up breaking them, which then gave the Dragon's Eye an excuse to arrest anyone they wanted to. If everyone was a criminal in one way or another, they could treat *anyone* like a criminal in one way or another. Some people—like his sister—thought that was unjust, but Abel was in middle school. Seventh grade was pretty much the same.

Still, Lina had leveled up from reading banned books to stealing dragons. That was *real* crime.

"Okay, team, let's harness these two big fellas and get out of here before the law shows up." Drey waved four of his Sky Knights minions to seize Karak and four more to seize Silas's wyvern. "Then toss these pilots off the roof."

"What? No!" Lina objected. "Captain! That is not the arrangement!"

"Ugh, right," Drey groaned. "I forgot. Your family. Sentimental thieves are the worst." He turned to his kinners. "Just tie these three up and leave them. Don't sulk! We'll go downtown and find some Red Talons to throw off a roof." The minions laughed, but when they moved toward Karak, the big dragon stopped their laughter with a roar.

Drey groaned and pulled a big sparkly necklace out of one of the many pockets of his coat. The necklace was a mixture of gold, diamonds, and rare shapes of natural dragon glass, the kind you could only find beyond the Glass Flats. It was probably worth more than a year's rent on Abel's family apartment. Probably more than a year's rent on every apartment in the building. He dangled it in front of Karak and the wyvern.

"You want this for your hoards?" he asked both dragons. "There's more like it too, if you come with us." He grinned at Lina. "I started out in the kin just like you, stealing dragons. Sometimes, this is all it takes."

The wyvern's eyes had gone wide with want; her huge forked tongue actually hung out, panting.

"Wondla, no," Silas groaned, but the dragon lowered her head to nuzzle Drey's whole body with her snout, a sign of submission. She was his now, and his minions were allowed to scurry onto her back, adjust her harnesses, and fly her off the roof.

Silas deflated like a week-old birthday balloon sitting on top of a trash can. Abel actually felt sorry for him.

Drey jingled the sparkling necklace in front of Karak. "Come on, Sunrise. You know you want this. It's yours if you're one of us . . ."

"Karak, forget this guy," Abel dared to say. Drey glared at him, and then at Lina with an *are-you-sure-I-can't-throw-your-brother-off-the-roof?* look.

Karak snorted, sparks leaping from his nose, and Abel felt a puff of pride. Unlike Silas's wyvern, his dragon was loyal.

"Of course, when this method doesn't work, there are other ways," Drey growled.

One of the minions behind Karak stepped forward with a big pole she unhooked from the Moss dragon's harness. It had a thick needle on the end, attached to a hose and air tank. With the push of a button, the needle shot forward, right between two of Karak's scales.

Abel's dragon screamed. Orange flame flared up in his throat, glowing between every seam of his scales and spine. His eyes blazed, and he reared up onto his back legs, wings spreading like a sheet of stars below a flaming sky. And then . . . nothing.

He sagged.

The flame faded, the glow between his scales turned white; his eyes too, and he settled calmly on the roof, staring straight ahead. The city lights danced on the pure whites of his unblinking eyes.

"It doesn't last long, but it'll be enough to take him away." Drey nodded at Lina. "You can handle it."

Her eyes lingered on Abel a moment, like she wanted to apologize. Instead, she turned back to her boss. "Savvy," she said. She climbed onto the ensorcelled dragon's back and goaded Karak to lift off. He moved like he was sleepwalking—or sleep-flying—but he obeyed.

The two black Half-Wyverns flanked Karak, using their own bodies to help lift the big reaper.

"Karak, wake up," Abel pleaded, but the dragon didn't or couldn't hear him.

"Sorry, kids," Drey said as he climbed back on his own Moss dragon. "But on the bright side, no one threw you off a roof!" He laughed and took off, vanishing into the colorful chaos of the city just before a huge spotlight hit the roof, gleaming bright as day.

"DO NOT MOVE," a mechanical voice shouted. "YOU ARE UNDER ARREST FOR TRESPASSING AND DESTRUCTION OF PROPERY. THIS IS A LAW ENFORCEMENT ACTION. DO NOT MOVE."

"Great timing, guys," Silas grumbled as a dozen wyverns circled them on the rooftop, a long-wing shining the spotlight down from high above.

"YOU ARE UNDER ARREST," the mechanical voice repeated. "DO NOT MOVE."

By the time Silas and Kai showed their Dragon's Eye identification to the police, Abel was already in handcuffs, facedown on the pavement.

He'd lost the dragon he was supposed to fly for the Thunder

Wings. His sister had escaped the Dragon's Eye, and probably broken their deal with the Red Talons. If Abel didn't end up in Windlee Prison before sunrise, he was definitely going to be grounded for the rest of his life.

IT WAS JUST AFTER SUNRISE when his parents picked him up from the fifty-seventh-floor landing plaza outside the Dragon's Eye Headquarters. Silas stood beside him in the morning sun, then passed him over to his parents' custody. He'd told his bosses at the Dragon's Eye that Lina had kidnapped her brother and used him as a hostage, and Kai backed the story up. It was the only thing that kept Abel out of an interrogation cell.

Now he had to keep the lie going, which would make Lina seem like a villain to their parents.

"She is a villain," Silas whispered to him, while his parents signed some paperwork for his release. "She's a kinner goon and a dragon thief. I never understood why you looked up to her."

"You mean instead of looking up to you?" Abel snapped back.

Silas elbowed him, hard, and shoved him toward Mom and Dad.

"What about Lina?" Dad said, his voice low. "Is she in custody? Is she safe?"

Silas snorted. "Your daughter is still at-large. There's a bounty on her now."

"You can't protect her anymore?" Dad said. "She's still your sister."

Silas just shook his head and walked back inside the headquarters.

Abel held his parents' hands like he was a little kid. "Mom, Dad, I'm sorry . . . I—"

"It's not your fault," his mother said, and ushered him toward the bus stop tower.

Except it *was* his fault. All of it. He'd been lying to them since the night Lina climbed through his window, and now he'd made everything worse. And he wasn't even in trouble for it, because they didn't know the truth. He would've felt better if he could at least get in trouble, if they'd yell at him or ground him. But his parents thought he was a *victim*. The guilt gnawed at him.

They didn't speak the entire time the number 27 express long-wing bus crossed the city, and they didn't speak when they transferred onto the short-wing local bus, a moody Greytoe dragon who wobbled with every breeze. It screeched at the traffic, which made Abel flinch each time. Then they *still* didn't speak on the entire walk from the drop-off tower to their apartment building.

As they passed Shivonne, still standing in the doorway to the laundromat with her paperback book, she gave Abel a sad smile. Behind her, Sax and Grackle glared at him and his parents hard enough to hammer a noodle into concrete.

When they finally got home, his father deflated just like Silas had when he'd lost his wyvern. He just kind of slumped onto the sofa. Percy padded over, climbed onto his lap, and rested his long snout there. When Dad didn't offer pats, Percy gently jabbed his long claws at his dad's knees. No reaction.

Abel's mother stood between the sofa and the kitchen.

"Lina . . . how could she?" she said. "And Silas? With the Dragon's Eye?" She shook her head. Abel wanted so badly to comfort her.

"I'm sorry, Mom. I—" he started again, but she just turned around and went to the fridge.

"I'll make pancakes," she said. She started taking out ingredients. She was still wearing her coat.

Normally, Abel loved his mother's pancakes. They were fluffy and tall and delicious, but he had no appetite. He didn't know what to do, but he knew he couldn't do it alone. The longer he stood staring at his mother cooking and his father zonked out, the worse he felt.

What would Dr. Drago do? he asked himself.

Not be a seventh grader, he answered himself.

This was too much for him. He had to come clean and hope that his parents had an idea how to help.

"Mom, stop cooking a sec," he said. "Dad, um . . . well . . . I have to tell you both something. I . . . well, you know the other night, when—"

Just then, his phone buzzed. It was a message from Roa.

WHERE ARE YOU?!

And then another:

EMERGENCY. CALL ME!

And then one from Instructor Ally that made him shudder:

Where is Karak? You better be on your way here now or in the belly of your dragon. If you're not here soon, you will be in the belly of ours.

"What is it, Abel?" his mother asked. "Are you hurt? Do you need to lie down?"

Suddenly, there was a pounding on the door so loud it made them all jump. His father stood. Percy curled into a ball and looked exactly like a throw pillow.

"Open up," Grackle barked at them. "We know you're home!"

"Don't make me smash your door with my boots," Sax added. "I don't want to scratch my new door-smashing boots."

Mom opened the door, and the two kinners strolled into the apartment like it was theirs. Sax had his hands in the pockets of his red leather jacket, and he whistled.

"You cleaned up real nicely since our last visit," he said, then kicked over the coatrack. It didn't break anything; it was just rude.

"Lina's not here," Dad said defiantly.

Grackle stomped across the living room and punched him right in the stomach, doubling him over. His father did his best to stand up straight again, his fists balled.

"Stop that!" his mom yelled. "Toliver, calm down; you'll get yourself killed."

He never heard his mom use his dad's name except when she was angry; sometimes it was the only way to know she *was* angry. She wheeled around on Sax and showed them how angry she was. "Can I offer you some tea while we talk?"

She didn't offer them cookies.

It wasn't much, but it was a small victory. She tossed the half-made pancake batter right in the trash and began making tea for the kinners. They ordered Abel to sit down next to his father on the couch. Sax sat in the chair opposite, glaring. Grackle went into Lina's room to rummage for clues.

"She's got a lot of banned books in here," he announced. "*The Soft Underbelly: An Upside-Down History of Drakopolis*. Sounds boring."

"She's got the entire Stone Street High School series too," Abel offered sarcastically. "You might like it. They're fantasy novels set in a world where there are no dragons and everyone's pretty and falling in love with each other all the time. Or living with rare diseases. Keep tissues handy, though; they'll make you cry."

Grackle popped out of the room, holding the first book in the series. "Really? I like a good cry."

"He's being a snot," Sax said. "Put the book back. We're not here for the library. We're here for Lina. Today's the day."

"But you can't!" Abel said. His parents glared at him urgently, trying to get him to stay quiet. He had to remind these goons that they'd *lost*, and that they were supposed to leave Lina alone now.

"You think there are *rules*, kid?" Sax laughed. "The only rule the Red Talons follow is power, and right now, we've got it and you don't. No Thunder Wings to protect you in here."

"What do the Thunder Wings have to do with anything?" his father asked.

"Ask your son." Sax grinned.

"We told you, we don't know where Lina is," his mother cut in, much to Abel's relief. She set two cups of tea on the little table. Grackle plodded over (still holding the young adult novel) and sat down on the couch next Abel and his dad. He sniffed the tea once.

"Claw flower?" he asked.

"With Sunberries," his mother said. That was their nicest tea, though Abel always thought it was too bitter. Grackle apparently did too. He dropped four sugar cubes in. Sax sipped his plain.

"Let's not play games," Sax said. "Your daughter stole from us, then broke an arrangement we had with the Dragon's Eye to make up for it. Now our boss is very angry."

"Surely the Red Talons have plenty of dragons to spare?" his mother suggested.

"The dragons we have or do not have are not your concern," Sax growled. "Your concern *should* be for your child, who took a very important dragon from one of our benefactors."

Abel frowned at his mother. He didn't know what a benefactor was.

"It's like a rich supporter," his father whispered to him.

"The blow to our finances was nothing compared with the blow to our pride," Sax said. "Our pride is wounded right now. And a wounded dragon is the most dangerous kind. They lash out. Entire buildings burn down. You don't want that to happen, do you? What would your neighbors say? Wouldn't you like to help us heal our wounded pride?"

"We'd help if we could," his mother said, sipping her own tea. Abel thought he detected a hint of mischief in her eyes. "But there's nothing *we* can do to help such a powerful kin like yours."

Sax ignored the sarcasm. "Call your daughter. Get her home. And maybe we can avoid having her torn limb from limb. If we find her on our own, well . . . it'll hurt worse for her. And as for you three . . ." He made a clicking sound with his teeth. "If she's not at the Half-Wing in the next two hours, Grackle and I have been ordered to start biting off fingers."

"Yours first," Grackle said, snapping his jaw at Abel.

"That's really gross," Abel replied.

"Don't yuck my yum," Grackle said. Then he lifted the young adult novel and began to read. "Anyway, we can wait."

He held out his cup for more tea without looking away from the book.

Abel's mother sighed and took the cup, then took Sax's too. She set them in the kitchen and came back empty-handed.

"Hey!" Grackle yelled. "I want *more* tea. Now!"

"You've had enough," Abel's mother said. "I don't want it to kill you."

"What?" The tuft of blue hair on top of Grackle's head twitched.

"Some time ago, Abel was prescribed a medicine for his distractibility," his mother said calmly. "The side effects were rather nasty, so we stopped using it, but I held on to what was left. You've each just had a rather large dose in your tea . . . and, well . . . it may cause—"

She pulled the small pill bottle from her coat pocket and read it to them. "Confusion, clumsiness, severe and sudden drowsiness. Do not operate any large dragons while taking."

"How did you— What did you—" Sax groaned, then tried to stand and tripped over his own ankle, falling back into his chair.

"That's the confusion and clumsiness," his mother said.

"You're in for trouble," Grackle growled. "You don't mess with the Red Tal—"

"And there's the sudden drowsiness," she said as the blue-haired kinner passed out.

Both Red Talons goons snored.

"This will buy us some time to think," his mother said, finally taking off her coat and setting the coatrack upright. Then she turned to Abel's dad. "Honeybreath," she said, using her cute nickname for him. "Would you please help me tie these two up? We'll have to use the bedsheets, but tomorrow's laundry day anyway."

Abel's dad nodded and stood.

"And, Abel," his mother said to him. "You should call your teacher and tell her you won't make it in to help her today."

"But it's Saturday," Abel objected. "I don't have to help her anyway! Why do I have to call?" He wasn't actually sure what the rules here were. With school being closed, were weekends not a thing anymore?

"I'd like you show her some courtesy," his mother said.

"I—" Abel was stunned that (a) his mother had just out-witted two kinners before 8:00 a.m., when most people had barely had their first cup of tea, and (b) that she was now tell-ing him to call the teacher who'd just threatened to feed him to a dragon if he didn't show up across town immediately. "Um—"

"I" and "um" were quickly becoming his most-used words. He really wished he had something better to say.

He pulled his phone out, just as it buzzed again. He was terri-fied to see what Instructor Ally and the Thunder Wings had to say now, but the text was from a blocked ID.

It was just an image, a picture of the same comic Lina had

given him where she'd hidden the keycard and the warehouse address. Except this time it was only the cover: Dr. Drago clutched in a wyvern's claws as he blasted at the Masked Rider with a laser pistol. The comic was still in its plastic sleeve, and written in marker right next to the price sticker from Chimera's All-Night Coffee + Comics was a time: just under an hour from now.

He recognized the handwriting. It was the same handwriting that had doodled hearts in the margins of the Stone Street High novel that now lay on the floor beside Grackle.

It was from Lina.

She wanted Abel to go the store. Was this how fugitives and secret agents set up meetings? Was it a trap or a peace offering?

The store wasn't that far away; he could make it on foot by cutting through the unmarked street with the fortune-teller on the corner. But how in the world was he supposed to do that? He couldn't leave home while his parents had two unconscious Red Talons tied up on the floor. He couldn't bail on Roa and Ally and the Thunder Wings without them coming after him either. And he also couldn't ignore his sister, who had *his* dragon.

How was he supposed to be in three places and satisfy three kins all at once?

And then he knew.

It was time. He had to do the unthinkable.

"Mom, Dad," he said. "I need your help."

Then Abel bit his lip, took a deep breath, and told them everything.

PART THREE

"CAKE'S BETTER THAN
VIOLENCE . . ."

21

EVERY EYE TURNED TO ABEL when he stepped through the door of Chimera's All-Night Coffee + Comics.

Behind the register, a tired-looking teen with more piercings than face sat up straight on his stool. The store's well-fed pangolin curled into a ball on the counter beside him. The barista in the café paused from the coffee she was whipping into a froth and looked Abel up and down over the rims of her rose-gold glasses. Her head was shaved, and a tattoo of a black dragon curled around a white wyvern decorated her scalp. She had different colored serpent rings on all her fingers.

The line of customers waiting for their coffee on the other side of the pastry case also looked at Abel. They were a colorful cross-section of every kind of person in the city, from the business people in suits to the students in hoodies and pajamas to the punks in every kind of thing imaginable, all of them united by a craving for early morning coffee and pastry.

There weren't a lot of customers in the bookshop section of the store this time of day, so he figured that's where he should go. The shelves were bursting with books—comics and novels and nonfiction. There were how-to guides on every topic imaginable, from telling fortunes with DrakoTek cards to the history of the glass trade in Drakopolis. There were picture books and young adult novels and an entire section of romances between humans and dragons labeled H/D, which seemed pretty weird to Abel, but that's what he loved about the store where his sister worked: there was something for literally everyone, even people whose lives and tastes were incomprehensible to him.

He wondered if Lina was here, watching from somewhere he couldn't see. If she was, she didn't reveal herself. He wandered down the first comic book aisle, acting interested in the new titles for the week. Then he realized he'd missed new comic day, and that he *was* actually interested. Abel pulled out the latest issue of *Sky Pirates*, a series about a group of outcasts from every kin in the city who unite to take on their former bosses and steal their riches to give to the poor and hungry. As he flipped through the issue, he found he couldn't focus. Maybe it was stress, or maybe reading made-up stories about kinners wasn't fun anymore, now that they were actually terrorizing him and his family in real life.

"You need help with something, kid? I've got good books on pirates all over the store. Histories, adventures, even how-tos."

Abel turned to see Fitz, the store's owner, right behind him. For a big guy, Fitz moved without making a sound. He had a huge smile and gave no hint that he'd seen Abel at the battle the night before. He did, however, hand Abel a bag with a sweet bean pastry in it.

"On the house," he said. "No one should browse hungry."

Abel smiled. He was starving. "Thanks."

"No wind off my tail." Fitz waved his thanks away. Unlike the kin leaders, Fitz was a guy who understood kindness.

Back when their dad was really sick, Abel and Lina had spent a lot of hours in this store, reading, listening to stories, learning about new bands, new authors, and new kinds of pastry, which Fitz sometimes let them taste for free. The café was famous for its creme-filled "dragon's teeth" and "sticky claw" buns. The shop was neutral territory for all the kin, so it was a safe place for Abel and Lina to spend their time when they weren't in school.

By the time their dad got out of the hospital, Lina had read half the books in the place, which was why Fitz hired her. He had a way of hiring all the neighborhood kids who needed it, but he somehow never seemed short on cash. Abel hadn't wondered about it before, but now that he knew his city was full of secrets, he wasn't sure he could trust Fitz. Half the time, he let people take books for free when he thought the book was just right for them. Even at thirteen, Abel knew that was no way to run a business.

"So, not interested in pirates today?" Fitz asked innocently. "A shame. You can learn a lot from pirates. My favorite was Mad Hazel the Marauder, who commanded a fleet of dragons that ruled the skies over half of Drakopolis five hundred years ago. She rode a dragon with a beautiful white mane of hair that was famous over the *whole* city. When she was finally caught, she braided her dragon's lovely mane with golden ribbon, put on her finest cloak and jewels, and commanded her dragon to burn down her own palace."

"She burned her own house down?" Abel shook his head. "Why?"

"I guess she'd rather see her riches burn than see them fall into her enemies' hands," Fitz said. "Or maybe pirates are just unpredictable?"

"Maybe," Abel said, not sure why Fitz was telling him this story.

"Anyway, you don't want pirates," Fitz said. "What are you looking for? I'm an expert at matching the right book to the right kid at the right time, you know?"

"I'm just . . . uh . . . browsing."

Fitz pursed his lips and nodded. "Fair enough. I'll mind my business." He looked around his store to make sure no one was eavesdropping on him—though, of course, someone was *always* eavesdropping. Any place that sold books would have at least one Dragon's Eye spy lurking about, and you never could tell who it was. "But if you're looking for a specific issue of Dr. Drago, you should know I'm sold out." He winked.

"Okay . . ."

"The customer who bought my last one just went across the street to the Drag On Lounge . . . if you wanted to talk to them about it. I think they're family."

"Family? Like—" Abel started.

"The family of comics fans." Fitz winked again, and Abel understood. His sister was across the street inside the Drag On Lounge. "If the bouncer gives you any trouble at the door because you're too young, just tell them Fitzy sent you."

And before Abel knew what was happening, Fitz had steered him outside.

"One more thing," Fitz told him. "They have a delicious green-tea milkshake. Don't leave without trying it." He patted Abel on the shoulder and disappeared back into his bookstore.

Abel stood blinking on the sidewalk in the morning

sunshine. It glittered and gleamed off the glass shopwindows all around.

Just then, a short-winged pink dragon glided right above him, nearly taking his head off with its foot. The pilot on the back shouted, "Watch it, short stuff!" like it was his fault. A Wingless Millifoot dragon scuttled by with a full cargo of deliveries on its long back and a sour-looking driver in the saddle by its shoulders. The dragon splashed Abel with the first twenty of its steps through a puddle before Abel was able to jump back. He suspected the driver had done that on purpose. People weren't polite this early in the morning in this part of town. Well, in *any* part of town.

The neon sign for the Drag On Lounge blinked and buzzed at him across the pavement. He brushed off his pant legs and strode over to it, looking side to side—and up—very carefully before he crossed. He tried to walk with as much confidence as he could, though he feared it was unconvincing.

He hoped his parents were doing okay with their part of the plan.

They'd hatched it this morning after he confessed everything.

Right about now, those Red Talons goons would be waking up in his apartment, bound and gagged, and his mom would be demanding a meeting with their boss. Dad was supposed to text Instructor Ally to get her to the same meeting. Abel had to arrange a meeting with *all* the kin leaders if his plan was going to work, and he was supposed to get Lina to invite the Sky Knights. He also needed his dragon back; he hoped Lina would help with that too.

Or he could be walking into another of her ambushes.

Either way, it was time to go inside. He'd never been inside a nightclub before, and he didn't know what happened there. *Is it still a nightclub if the sun is up?*

• • •

As promised, once he said Fitz had sent him, the bouncer let him in, even though there was a glowing sign that said NO CHILDREN ALLOWED. It had a dragon eating a little baby on it and part of it was flickering and buzzing. It was such an old sign the little neon baby on it would be a neon adult by now.

Inside, the club was dimly lit and nearly empty. There were round booths with red velvet seats spread around the edge of a huge semicircular room, facing a stage that took up an entire wall. Lush green velvet curtains hung along the back of the stage, with gold curtains off to the side. Abel could see that one of those curtains covered the door to a janitor's closet, which kind of ruined the illusion of luxury.

"Find a seat, kid! The morning show's about to start!" a host yelled, waving him toward the booths. The host was dressed in a dark suit and their long hair was tied into a ponytail. They looked pretty unremarkable, except that their face was painted with elaborate makeup that looked just like a dragon's face.

Suddenly, something jostled Abel from behind. A drake—an undersized dragon—trundled past. It had purple scales and golden feet but was dressed to look like a person in a tuxedo, complete with a black bow tie and four little sleeves down its four legs. It had a silver tray strapped to its back and was carrying two bright green milkshakes.

Don't leave without trying it, Fitz had told him. That wasn't a suggestion; it was a hint!

He followed the trained dragon waiter to an empty booth in a shadowy corner and took a seat as the dragon rested one wing on the table and tilted to the side so the milkshakes could slide onto the table. It didn't spill a drop.

"Thank you," Abel said, mindful of a dragon's pride. It made a snorting sound and padded away. The lights dimmed. A spotlight hit the stage.

A pop song burst from the speakers, an old hit about a person in love with someone from a different kin. The beat thumped as the lyrics began.

> *Our gang's at war, but I love you more*
> *Than any dragon loves her hoard.*
> *The skies are on fire, with my burning desire*
> *For youuuuu . . . for youuuu . . . for YOUUUU!*

On the last "YOUUUU" a golden curtain fluttered, and the performer strode onto the stage like a vision from a dream.

They were human but dressed and made up to look like a huge and glorious Dazzler dragon, with wings of bejeweled cloth and a sequin dress of rainbow scales. Their boots had heels so high they made Abel dizzy to look at them, and they were covered in tiny mirrors that caught the spotlight and refracted it into a thousand rainbows all over the empty club. Even though they were human, they had captured the feeling of a rare Dazzler dragon perfectly. They spread their arms wide in front of their grand wings and lip-synched the next verse with such passion it made Abel's belly button tingle. He'd never seen a performance like this.

Bare your teeth and show your claws!
For you, I'll break my jail cell's walls!
I'll be your dragon queen,
greater than you've ever seen!
Your Dragon Queen!
Your Dragon Queen!

"Her stage name is Raina Terror," Lina said, sitting down at the table opposite Abel without even saying hello. Where had she come from? "She's great, right?"

"Um . . ." Abel feared "um" was officially his catchphrase.

"Just be cool," Lina said. "I asked her to perform this morning, because she's so good no one can look away."

"So no one will look at us," Abel said. "Smart."

"Thanks," Lina replied. "And thanks for meeting me. I'm sorry about last night. I had to get Karak back."

"You didn't *have* to," Abel said, taking a big sip of his milkshake. It *was* really good. "You *chose* to."

Lina tapped the rim of her glass. "Following orders is one of the first lessons you learn in the Sky Knights."

"I guess you let their lessons make less of you," Abel said, remembering what the hostess at the laundromat-casino had said to him.

"I did what?" Lina frowned. "Is that some line from a comic?" She shook her head, changing the subject. "Here's the problem: There's a kin battle coming up, and I was supposed to battle with Karak for the Sky Knights . . . But he won't let me ride him now."

"Maybe your boss shouldn't have stuck that poison in him after all?"

"I don't approve of what Drey did, but he had to act quickly before the cops showed up."

"It's not right to treat a dragon that way," Abel said. "It's cruel. And it offends them. Karak is very sensitive to good manners."

"I know that," Lina told him. She played with the straw in her milkshake but didn't take a sip. Onstage, Raina Terror was twirling in circles and dancing so that her huge wings flapped and caught the light at different angles, painting the walls all around with light. "Karak is loyal . . . to *you*. He chose you, Abel, and we need *you* to fly him for us."

"What?" Abel almost snorted green milkshake from his nose.

"We have to win this next battle," Lina said. "We need more dragons. The Red Talons are too powerful, and they're plotting to take over more neighborhoods. If they do that, it'll start a war, one no one can win. If we can get more of their dragons, maybe they'll think twice about a conflict and we can keep peace in the city."

Abel grunted. "Some peace this is," he said. "What's the difference between one gang of kinners or another controlling a neighborhood? It's not like any of the kins are the good guys."

"*We're* good guys," Lina said. "The Sky Knights are good guys. We're not just kinners. We're"—she lowered her voice—"revolutionaries."

Abel frowned.

"Come with me," she said. "I'll show you."

She got up from the table and walked toward an emergency exit door in the corner of the club. Lina didn't look back to see if Abel was following; she just assumed he was, because she was his big sister and she knew he was curious and that he wanted his dragon back.

He hated that she was right.

He took one more gulp of the milkshake and one more look at the dragon performer on the stage, pretending to belt out a song of heartbreak. Then he followed his fugitive sister into the alley, hoping she hadn't planned another ambush.

IT WAS AN AMBUSH, **B**UT not the kind he'd feared.

Lina had a short-wing Blue Foot dragon waiting in the alley for them to ride. The Blue Foot was one of the more common dragons around the city. They didn't have a breath weapon, and they came in all kinds of colors, except for their feet, which were always . . . yeah . . . blue. If you wanted to fly around without anyone paying attention, a Blue Foot was the dragon for the job.

Abel hesitated, but Lina assured him it would be okay. She just wanted to give him a look at something she was sure he'd never seen before.

"And then you'll take me to Karak?" he asked.

"I will," she said.

"Swear it," Abel said.

"You don't trust me?"

Abel tried to raise an eyebrow at her, though he wasn't very good at it. He probably just looked confused, but she got the point.

"I swear," she said.

"On a secret," he added. "Swear on . . . Kai Parchuli?"

"Kai . . . how did you—you read my diary!" Lina gasped.

Abel just shrugged. "You've got my dragon. I needed leverage."

Kai Parchuli, it turned out, wasn't just Silas's partner. He had been Lina's crush since elementary school. She'd written about Kai in long, flowery paragraphs like she was describing the hero of one of her young adult novels. Kai's hair. Kai's eyes. The way Kai's obscure band T-shirts hung off Kai's dark shoulders.

It was nauseating, but also appropriately embarrassing if Kai ever found out.

"I wrote an email with screenshots to automatically send to Silas if I don't cancel it," Abel said. "Just to make sure I get home safely."

He thought Lina would be mad, but she actually laughed. "That's real smart of you, little bro," she said. "I mean, *awful* of you too, and I'm definitely going to have to get revenge some-day. But still . . . clever. You might be a criminal mastermind after all."

"I don't want to be a criminal mastermind," Abel said.

"Good," Lina replied. "Because neither do I. Let's go."

He got into the harness behind Lina. She nudged the dragon forward and into the air to join the midmorning city traffic.

They turned onto a huge boulevard that ran in a spiral pattern, from city hall in the center all the way out to the farms and Glass Flats beyond, slicing through just about every neighbor-hood on its way. There was always traffic in every direction on the Spiral Boulevard, central street of Drakopolis, though Lina merged effortlessly into it, her little dragon slipping between two green long-wing dragons with cargo containers on their backs. A medium-winged Orange Stalker glided above them, and they fell into its shadow.

Suddenly, the two green dragons squeezed in close on either

side, blocking their view of the rest of the traffic. A rope dropped down from the cargo basket the dragon above them had on its belly.

"We have to switch rides real fast," Lina said. "In case we're being followed."

A girl who looked just like Lina and was dressed just like Lina slid down the rope and landed on their dragon's back, taking the reins. Lina scurried up the rope just as quickly. When she got to the top, a boy dressed just like Abel slid down and smiled at him, then flashed him the infinity sign with his hands. When Abel just stared blankly, Lina whisper-shouted, "Abel, come on!"

Despite being in the middle of moving traffic, high in the swirling boulevard, Abel scurried up the rope. His feet and hands tingled with fear until he was safely enclosed in the dark cargo basket. The moment he was inside, he peered out the breathing holes and saw the two green dragons break away in opposite directions, while the Blue Foot dropped to a lower level of traffic. The dragon that carried them flew steady on its same course.

"Evasive maneuvers," Lina said. "One of the first things the Sky Knights taught me."

"How did that boy have clothes like mine?" Abel wondered.

"You wear the same two things every day," Lina said. "I took the clothes from your room."

"How long *have* you been a kinner thief?" Abel asked.

Lina smiled. "Since the day Silas went to the Academy," she said. "I figured someone had to counteract the harm he'd do serving the City Council."

"But that's the government," Abel said. "They run the city and keep it safe. And you were only a little kid then yourself!"

"I was old enough to know something is wrong in Drakopolis," she said. "That the City Council doesn't serve the people. They serve the powerful. I wanted to change things. That's why I joined the Sky Knights. We aren't like the other kins. We aren't in it for territory or money or power. We're not criminals. We're fighting to free everyone, whether they know it or not."

"Not everyone," Abel said. "You stole Karak and hijacked Silas's wyvern. *They* aren't free."

"Every *human*, Abel," Lina grunted. "Grow up. Anyway, we're more like the sky pirates in your comics. We steal for the good of the community. I'll show you."

Their dragon left the main boulevard and flew its way through the winding streets of Drakopolis, until they reached a tall apartment building that looked like hundreds of others. It had a big Sky Knights symbol spray-painted on the side of one of its landing zones, and that's where the dragon dropped them off.

• • •

Inside the apartment building was not an apartment building.

As Lina led Abel through the halls, he saw that there were offices for the Sky Knights, and training rooms, and weapons lockers, and even a day care. She took him up in the elevator to a medical clinic where people got treatment for everything from dragon burns to upset stomachs, free of charge.

"This is not what I was expecting from a kin headquarters," he said.

"Where do you think I got Dad his Scaly Lung pills half the time?" Lina told him. "We run a food pantry on an upper floor, and there's a free library too. This is just one of our buildings. We have centers like this all over the neighborhoods we control. We use our winnings from the kin battles to help people."

Abel looked at the medical staff in their face masks with the Sky Knights emblem stenciled on. He looked at the graffiti on the walls that didn't just have the kin symbol, but also sayings like *Freedom isn't given by the powerful, it is taken by the free* and *A dragon's wings are useless without its claws*. The sayings were supposed to be inspiring, but they also felt kind of threatening. He couldn't figure out why *he* felt threatened by them, though. Maybe it was the guards in Sky Knights colors who stood all over the place, watching everyone from behind dark sunglasses.

"See that little girl there?" His sister pointed at a sickly-looking girl on a plastic chair, waiting her turn to see the nurse. Lina went over and gave her a ginger candy, ruffling her hair and making her laugh. She pulled a comic book out—the new issue of *Sky Pirates*—and gave it to the girl, before coming back to Abel.

"Her parents got in trouble with the Red Talons," she said when she'd returned. "They went to the Dragon's Eye, like they were supposed to. Instead of protecting them, the Dragon's Eye looked the other way, told them to mind their business. *Then* they told the Red Talons that the family had snitched on them. Her parents lost their jobs, got chased out of their home, and came to us for help. We didn't turn them away. We don't turn anyone away. All we ask in return is that those who can fight help us fight."

"But what about people who don't want to be revolutionaries?" Abel said. "Or who live in another kin's territory?"

"Everyone has a role to play in the revolution," Lina said. "If someone has the chance to be with us and chooses not to, then they're against us . . . and we deal with our enemies."

"That's harsh," Abel told her.

"Freeing the people of Drakopolis from tyranny is hard," she told him. "We have to be selfless and brave, which means putting aside our own feelings to serve the Sky Knights' revolution. We're raised to think stealing is wrong. But which is more wrong—stealing a dragon from the powerful to help feed people, or letting those people starve?"

He thought about Topher, how the Thunder Wings made him work for *them* just because his mom had obeyed the law and snitched. Now he saw how the Sky Knights helped people, but expected those people to fight for them in return. It didn't seem fair either. Help that came with conditions like that wasn't kindness. It was just another trade.

"You really make people join your cause in order to get medicine and food?" Abel asked her.

"Not all sickness is in the body, and not all hunger is in the belly," Lina said, and tapped her finger on the side of her head. "Think about it. The people's *minds* are starving for freedom, even if they don't know it. We make them see."

"Okay, so you've got a lot of big ideas," Abel said. "But that doesn't make hijacking my dragon right."

"I'm going to take you to Karak," she said. "He's just a few floors up from here . . . But there's something I want you to do, now that you've seen what the Sky Knights really are."

"What's that?" he asked.

"I want you to help *our* dragon win," she said. "I want to you to lose your next battle on purpose."

"I don't have a next battle," Abel said.

"You will," Lina said. "I know you."

"But then you'd win Karak," Abel told her.

"We already *have* Karak. We could just keep him," she said. "He'll eventually let another rider fly him, if we're patient. But we want to win the Red Talons' dragon . . . and the Thunder Wings' too. We need to win them all."

"So you want me to cheat," Abel said. "Even if it means losing my dragon *again* and getting in trouble with all the other kin?"

"Selflessness demands sacrifice," Lina said. "The cause is more important than any of us."

She made the infinity symbol with her hands, then led him to some concrete stairs. They ascended a few floors to a huge ballroom, with high ceilings and three crystal chandeliers. It had one entire wall open to the sky.

Karak was curled around a fourth crystal chandelier on the floor, sleeping soundly. But when Abel came into the room, his snout twitched and his eyes slitted open. He sat up so fast his head smacked the plaster ceiling, raining dust. The dragon sneezed sparks. He had a heavy chain around his neck and two more around his back paws.

"You *chained* him?" Abel said, distraught.

"We had to," Lina said. "But we made him comfortable. Gave him a big meal."

There were fast food wrappers all around, enough to fill a bus.

"You gave him *tacos*?"

Lina nodded. "After the serum wore off. He was pretty angry at us, and we had to calm him down. He loves tacos."

The dragon let out a snort.

"I think he's still angry," Abel said.

"Like I said, I don't approve of what Drey did to subdue him, but we needed to do it. We couldn't let him fall into anyone else's hands, especially not the Dragon's Eye."

"But now you're just giving him back to me?" Abel was suspicious.

She handed him another keycard and pointed to a panel on the wall. "Swipe it against that. It'll unlock the chains, and you two can go. No one will try to stop you."

"I didn't agree to throw a battle for you," Abel reminded her.

"I know," Lina told him, backing toward the door to the stairs. She clearly didn't want to be there when his dragon was unchained. "I know you, Abel. And I know you'll do the right thing."

After she was gone, Abel patted Karak's snout gently. He wished he knew what the right thing was anymore.

IT WAS LUNCHTIME AND ABEL was hungry, so it was good he got a text from his mom telling him that lunch was ready at the Half-Wing Diner.

The message was a code they'd agreed on earlier: It meant he should pick up Karak and his dad, who had Grackle as a hostage, then stash them in a safe place. His mother had taken Sax with her to the diner for a sit-down with all the kin leaders. The code meant she was there safe.

If she hadn't been, she would've texted him to fix his own lunch. It was a simple code, but that's what made it so smart. It was just the kind of thing a mom *would* text to her kid, even if there were no kinners or secret police watching them.

Luckily, Abel had an idea about just where he could stash his father, a kinner hostage, and a stolen ten-ton Sunrise Reaper where no one would look. With his dad and Grackle strapped into the saddle behind him, he flew across the city, keeping to the low lanes and back alleys as much as possible. His dad kept trying to pilot from behind him, and it wasn't until Karak gave him some serious dragon side-eye that he zipped his lips and let his son fly him to safety.

Once Abel saw the laughing dragon of the Wind Breakers kin on the side of the half-ruined skyscraper, he knew he was in the right place.

He landed on one of the high floors, and the people inside scattered at the sight of the huge Reaper. They had tents that lined what used to be office cubes, and they'd turned what had been offices into shared kitchens and playrooms. There were no sayings on the walls here, or guards peering at anyone. From what he knew about the Wind Breakers kin, they had no leaders or rules. Their only goal was chaos. That's what everyone said. They were called terrorists, though he couldn't think of a single time they'd hurt anyone. Even the attack on his school had been faked by the Sky Knights. The Wind Breakers only disrupted things; they didn't destroy them.

He was betting everything on them wanting to help him disrupt a kin battle.

"Hello?" he called out. Eyes peered out at him from hiding spots as wind rustled through the hanging laundry and sparks hissed from loose wires. "Um . . . I'm a friend of Shivonne's?" he tried, remembering her secret Wind Breakers tattoo. "And this is my dad and Karak."

His dad climbed down, leaving Grackle tied up in the harness, looking sour. He had Percy snuggled in his arms.

"What?" his dad said. "I couldn't just leave him!"

Abel, his father, and the pangolin waited. The people stayed hidden. They were afraid.

"We need . . ." He tried to think of the right word. Something that would show he wasn't coming here demanding anything, but that he was asking for help. Even though he had a terrifying dragon standing behind him with a ball of bright red flame glowing like a rising sun at the back of his throat, the people were free to say no. He wanted them to have a choice.

"Sanctuary," he said at last.

Dragons are powerful, he thought, *but power is complicated to have. And not to have. Having dragons, then, is complicated.*

So he waited more. He had to give them time to think, time to decide if he was someone they could trust. Whatever they decided to do, it wasn't up to him to command them, even if he could. That's not the kind of person he wanted to be. Like Shivonne had said, *The city will teach you hard lessons. Don't let them make less of you.*

He reached back and placed a hand on Karak's chest, calming the dragon's building mouthful of fire. After a few long minutes with only the sound of Karak's rumbling breaths and the wind howling through the open walls for answers, Abel decided the people must've been too afraid. He couldn't really blame them. If he could've avoided the attention of all the kins and the Dragon's Eye, he would've too.

He turned to go, trying to think of a new plan, someplace else they could hide out.

"Wait," a voice called. An older woman emerged, with long braids of gray hair tied back with copper wire that was probably stripped from the walls of this very building. Her long dress blew in the wind.

She came forward, her bare arms open. She had the kind of face that Abel imagined a goddess in a storybook would have— wizened but also hardened, kind but not nice, with dark eyes that were sharp and clear. However, when she spoke, she sounded nothing like he thought a goddess would. "Y'all can stay, but that big fella there best not eat my cakes."

Behind her, people started to come out from hiding, pulling

back curtains and tent flaps. Abel saw a table laid out with cakes in all different sizes and colors. There were so many they made his mouth water.

"He's a charivore," Abel explained. "He won't eat your cakes unless they're burned, and you look like too good a baker for that."

The woman frowned. Abel worried he shouldn't have a made a joke, but then she burst out laughing and welcomed him to what she called their "neighborhood cooperative." Her name was Sippa and she lived there with her eight sons and their families, and several other families, though she was eldest and the best baker, which she said gave her some authority to make decisions for the group.

"Cake's better than violence for picking leaders." She smiled. She pulled a treat out of her pocket and let Percy nibble from her palm. Karak eyed the tiny pangolin with jealousy.

Still, she explained, if the others objected to Abel's dragon taking sanctuary with them, he had to go.

More people came out, maybe fifty in all, of all ages. Abel had to present his case.

"So the kin are after us," he said, "and the Dragon's Eye. My family and I are trying to do something about all that, but we need a safe place to lie low until we can, and this is the only place I could think of. I don't know where else to go."

The people murmured to one another and then, with a simple show of hands, they had a vote. They agreed unanimously that Karak, his dad, and their hostage could stay.

Abel's dad beamed at him, like he'd just gotten a good grade on a book report.

"It's only for a little while," Abel told them all. "I'll be back just as soon as I sort some stuff out with—"

"We don't want to know," Sippa cut him off. "Your business is your business. We're on no government maps and pledge no loyalty to any kin. All we ask is you keep it that way. Anyone comes asking for you, our mouths are shut. But you better return that same courtesy to us. That's how we stay invisible here. No one talks."

"That's just what I was hoping for," he told them gladly, and helped get Karak settled in an open space deeper in the building where he couldn't be seen by any dragons flying by outside. There was a big pile of old pipes and scrapped computer parts and salvaged junk from all over the skyscraper.

"We trade with other floors and other buildings like this one," Sippa explained. "This is the junk no one wants. It's not worth much to us, but it's shiny."

"Will this be okay?" Abel asked his dragon. Karak answered by thundering across the floor and climbing atop the pile of junk, turning three times in a circle and settling down to rest on the garbage heap with a contented, smoky sigh. "Guess he likes it," Abel said, and thanked Sippa and her family again for letting them stay. "And you'll be all right?" he asked his dad.

"Just fine," Abel's dad said, pushing Grackle into a corner beside Karak's pile of junk. "Don't worry about us. Go meet your mother."

"Okay, then," Abel said. "I'll be back as soon as I can."

"Take your time," his father said. He smiled at Sippa. "I'd love to hear more about these cakes."

Abel made his way down two hundred flights of stairs to the ground level. He had a bus to catch and a meeting to get to. His mother and the leaders of the most ferocious dragon-battling kin in the city were all waiting for him.

He hoped there was lunch.

24

THE HALF-WING DINER WAS ON the top floor of a dirty old building down a side street off the Spiral Boulevard. The building had a historic plaque on it because it was the place, three hundred years ago, where a famous stage actress was eaten by her own pet wyvern. Because of that plaque, the building could never be torn down or fixed up or changed in any way, which meant it slowly decayed over time. The apartments inside were abandoned, and no one visited the place.

That was why the Red Talons used it for their headquarters. It wasn't the sort of building where outsiders would feel welcome, and the diner wasn't the sort of restaurant where outsiders would want to eat.

Just like when he'd entered Chimera's All-Night Coffee + Comics, every head in the place turned to look at Abel.

At every table, there were kinner goons. There were goons in Red Talons colors with Red Talons tattoos, and goons in Thunder Wings colors with Thunder Wings tattoos, and goons in Sky Knights colors with Sky Knights tattoos. And they were all glaring at Abel.

At one table, he saw Instructor Ally, frowning at him. She shook her head ever so slightly, like she did whenever Topher was gearing up to say something in class that was sure to get him in trouble. Abel had never been on the receiving end of that look before, and he didn't like it.

Sax was at another table, and he shook his head at Abel like he was threatening to eat him. That was a look Abel knew by now. He didn't like it either.

"Hi, Abel!" his mother called out, waving from a booth in the back. It was weird seeing her in this place, but weirder still was the company with her. Their table was framed by a huge curved window, which would've had a lovely view of the city, except it was so stained and dirty that the outside world looked more like a greasy blur.

In front of that blur sat the leaders of the three biggest kin. There was Olus Eisink, the leader of the Thunder Wings, whom Abel knew already. Next to him was Captain Drey, whom Abel also, unfortunately, knew already. And then, closest to his mother, the one leader he hadn't yet had the misfortune to meet, but whom he'd grown up hearing stories about—Jazinda Balk, current leader of the Red Talons. She'd been in charge since Abel was three years old, when she had the previous leader melted by the breath of their own dragon, which she had secretly trained against them.

She was from a famous family of kinners, all of whom were either dead or in Windlee Prison.

"I ordered you some mixed buns," his mother said as he sat down. An elderly waiter slammed a steaming plate in front of him.

"Thank you," Abel said.

"There're not poisoned," the waiter snarled as he walked away.

"Um, I didn't think they were?" Abel said. Though now, of course, he did. Then again, if Jazinda Balk wanted him dead, she could've already done it. And he really was so hungry. So he picked one up, took a bite, and smiled at the scowling kin bosses in front of him. "Yum."

"Nice of you to show up to your own meeting," Jazinda said to him, weaving her long fingers together on the table in front of her. "We're not used to being kept waiting, especially not by children."

She was wearing a bright red jumpsuit with intricate light red stitching and a necklace of carved jade dragons that looked even more expensive. She had a ring of scars dotting her entire neck. Abel noticed that the scars were all slightly different sizes, in a very specific and very familiar order. They looked like a row of dragon's teeth. Had a dragon once tried to bite Jazinda's head off?

And had it *failed*?

"Sorry I'm late," Abel said insincerely. "Did I miss anything?"

Jazinda smiled at him, also insincerely. "You have our stolen dragon," she said. "Return it."

"It's *our* stolen dragon," Olus said, setting his heavy palms flat on the table in front of him. He had tattoos of different tools laid out in a neat row from just behind his knuckles all the way up his forearms. The man really liked tools. "Return it to us."

"I believe we were both the first *and* the last to steal it," Drey said. He looked a lot younger than he had the night before, when he was threatening to throw Abel off a roof. "Any claim on the dragon should belong to the Sky Knights."

"Technically," Abel said, "*I'm* the last one to steal it, so any claim on it is *mine*. Finders keepers, right?" He grinned. "But you can win it from me. This is a challenge." He knocked the table with his knuckles. He didn't know if that was a thing you did to issue a challenge, but it felt right.

The kin leaders all grunted and grumbled, but Jazinda actually broke into a real smile. "So you're making a challenge? You want to fly your Sunrise Reaper for a kin. Very good." She knocked her knuckles on the table too. "The question is, for which kin?"

"For us," the other two kin leaders said in unison.

"We trained him," Olus said.

"His sister's one of ours," Drey said.

"But he owes us," Olus replied.

"And *she* owes *us*," Jazinda added. "For stealing the dragon in the first place."

"And you burst into our home and threatened my family," Abel's mother said. She showed not even the slightest sign of fear, though she and Abel were the only non-kinners in the diner, if not the entire 150-story building. "So *you* owe *us*."

All three kin leaders laughed.

"The mama dragon is fierce," Jazinda said. "As a parent myself, I like to see that. Maybe I'm sentimental. I *should* have had your whole family eaten by a toothless dragon by now."

"Why toothless?" Abel wondered.

"Because it would hurt more." Jazinda beamed a smile that sent a chill up his spine. "But instead, I'm giving you the opportunity to fly the Sunrise Reaper for the Red Talons kin. After you win, you will surrender the dragon, and all will be forgiven."

"If he flies for you, that's an act of war," Olus said.

"Agreed," Drey added. "The peace between the kins will be broken."

"You call this peace?" Abel couldn't believe it. "Your battles trash entire neighborhoods, you break into people's homes and threaten them, and you're constantly stealing from each other . . . and from everyone else!"

"So just imagine what a war would be like," Jazinda said. "We don't want one, but we'd win one if it started."

"Maybe it already has started," Drey said.

"Is that a threat?" Jazinda replied.

"Just an observation," Drey said.

"The Thunder Wings don't want a war," Olus told them all. "We just want what's ours. We'll give up our claim on the boy *and* his dragon in exchange for control of . . ." He rubbed his chin. "The 1700 block of the Northwest Downs neighborhood."

"That's *our* block!" Abel exclaimed as Olus chuckled.

"Is it? Well, I hope none of my people hold a grudge against you for betraying us. These young kinners are so unpredictable with their tempers. You might want to be careful on your way to school."

"No deal," said Jazinda. "We're not giving up any turf to you and your geeks."

"The Sky Knights will give up their claim on the boy and his dragon in exchange for your help with the Dragon's Eye," said Drey. "We know you work with them. They've arrested some of our operatives, and we want them released from Windlee."

"Definitely no deal," Jazinda said. "We have a good relationship with the Dragon's Eye *because* we never ask for favors like that."

"Then we're at an impasse," Drey said.

"Agreed," Olus said. "He flies for anyone, then the others will go to war."

"Then he should fly for no one," Abel's mother said. "Forget about him, and there's no need for war."

They all laughed again.

"No," Jazinda said.

"Not an option," Olus said.

"No chance," Drey added.

"You have to understand our situation." Jazinda leaned toward his mother, jade necklace gleaming in the soft light through the greasy window. "We've all been robbed. Your family has wronged each of the kins in one way or another, and none of us can let that go unanswered. It's the way of things. The moment your daughter stole from us and your son stole from her, your family's options dwindled. Your son will *need* to fly for one of the kins because your family needs protection from all the others now. And the Red Talons, I assure you, are the kin you most want on your side and that you least want against you." She turned her attention to Abel. "Fly for us."

Abel gazed around the table. There were no good options with any of the kins, and there was no way he could do what his sister wanted—lose on purpose. He took a bite out of one of the buns on the plate in front of him, stalling. It was hot and greasy and he really wished he could enjoy it, but he was just searching for the nerve to speak.

WW3D, he told himself. *WW3D*.

His mother put a hand on his, reassuring him. This was their plan, but she couldn't do this part for him. He had to sell the idea on his own.

"I won't fly for you," he announced. Jazinda frowned, and all around the diner, her goons tensed. Olus and Drey leaned forward, eager. Their goons also tensed. "I won't fly for any of you," he clarified. "But I challenge *all* of you."

"You can't," Drey said.

"We only take challenges from other kins," Olus said. "And you are still just a civilian."

"I'm challenging all of you on behalf of . . ." He paused for dramatic effect. ". . . the Wind Breakers kin."

Jazinda just tapped her fingers on the table in front of her.

"They don't battle," Drey said.

"You're not one of them," Jazinda said.

"They have no rules," Abel explained. "Anyone who pledges loyalty to disorder and chaos and the wildness of the dragons can fly with them. And look at what I've done. Since the moment I first stepped into the warehouse where my sister stashed Karak, it's been chaos for all of you. I'm an agent of chaos, whether I like it or not. So I have every right to challenge you under the name of the Wind Breakers kin."

Olus's eyes narrowed, thinking. "That tracks," he said.

Drey sucked his teeth. "Interesting," he said.

"If we accept this challenge," Jazinda said, "you'd need to make the bet worth it for us." She looked around the table at the other kin leaders. "For *all* of us. And what could a little boy with a sick father and a mother who works at a dragon feed factory have that we want? You and your family are nobodies."

"That doesn't mean we're worthless," Abel said. "Whoever

gets my hoard in the battle, gets Karak. And . . ." He looked at his mother. This was her part.

"And access to the dragon feed at my factory," she said. "Unlimited and free. I supervise the loading dock. I can make sure that several tons go missing every week."

"You'd steal? A nice working lady like yourself would turn thief?" Jazinda looked amused.

"We don't need your stolen food," Olus said. "The Thunder Wings have access to our own food supplies."

"That's the other part of my offer," his mom said. "You also have a lot of investigations open into your members, wanted by the Dragon's Eye for a lot of crimes. If my son loses—"

"When," Sax grumbled from a nearby table.

"*IF my son loses,*" his mother repeated loudly, without turning to look at the kinner she'd knocked out with poisoned tea just a few hours earlier, "my husband will turn himself in to the Dragon's Eye. He'll confess to whatever crimes the winner needs someone to confess to. It will let your actual criminals off the hook."

The table fell silent. Abel's stomach knotted.

Jazinda narrowed her eyes. "That is an interesting proposal. Do you realize what you're offering?"

"We do," his mother said.

Abel's dad, who wasn't in the best health to begin with, was offering to take the fall for the kin's worst crimes? He could spend the rest of his life in jail for things he didn't do.

"The Sky Knights don't turn people over to the Dragon's Eye," Drey said. "We don't like this offer."

"We'll take it," Olus said.

"We will too," Jazinda agreed.

Drey sighed. "Ma'am—"

"Call me Graselle," his mother said, like they were becoming friends.

"Graselle," Drey said. "I don't think your daughter would appreciate what you're doing. She believes in *justice*."

"With respect, Drey?"

"Captain Drey," he corrected her. Once, he'd been a real captain in the Aerial Brigade.

"Well, *Captain* Drey, with all due respect"—she folded her fingers on the table in front of her and leaned forward in a way that made it pretty obvious she didn't think any respect was due—"I won't be lectured about justice by a kinner who terrorizes our city." She leaned back. "The others have agreed. You should too."

Drey sucked his teeth, considering. "Fine," he said at last. "The cause can make use of your husband's confessions. But I warn you—they will be *plentiful*."

"Good," said Abel's mom. Then she turned to him with a nod.

"The flip side of this," Abel said, "is that when I win, not only do I get all the other dragons to do with as I please." He paused and took another bite of the steamed bun in front of him, making them all watch and wait as he chewed. It felt like a power move. Sometimes having power meant relinquishing it, but sometimes it demanded to be used. He chewed slowly, using every bit of power he felt he had. Turned out, he liked feeling powerful. "You all will forgive my family for everything that's happened. We win, we don't owe any of you anything else."

"Whatever," said Olus.

"Sure thing, kiddo," said Drey.

"Fine," said Jazinda, with the sort of cold smirk that made Abel think she didn't really mean it. None of them thought he could win anyway.

"Then it's set," Jazinda said. "Tomorrow night at midnight, the kin will gather for this challenge. Winner takes all. Someone please send a message to Fitz that his services are required, for the usual fee, of course." Everyone around the table nodded in agreement. Jazinda rapped her knuckles on the tabletop a final time. "Savvy. Now all of you get out of my diner."

Abel's mom took his hand and squeezed it again. He was glad their plan had worked. The problem was . . . their plan had worked.

Abel was going up against all the kins, with less than a week of training and one grumpy dragon to his name.

He had to convince his best friend to join him.

"No, no, no," **Roa said,** their arms folded in front of them as they sat on the end of their bed. Abel's mom was in the living room with Roa's parents, letting him and his friend have some privacy while he pleaded his case.

"Look, you saw what Ally did to her own Yellow Stinger," Abel said. "Just because the Thunder Wings are your kin doesn't mean they have to *stay* your kin. They're not, like, family."

"You know that's literally what 'kin' means, right?" Roa said. "The word 'kin' means 'family.'"

"Families don't treat each other the way these kin do," Abel replied.

"You're not one to lecture me about families," Roa snapped at him. "Your sister's a thief and your brother's a Dragon's Eye agent. At least the Thunder Wings taught me to heal dragons. They taught *you* everything you know about flying one."

"To be fair, I don't know much," Abel joked, but Roa was in no mood for humor. Neither was Abel, really, but joking was the best alternative he could think of to pleading and crying.

"Even if they hadn't taught me anything," Roa said, "I took an oath to them, and if I break it, what does that say about me? Plus, I live in Thunder Wings territory. If I betray them, my family won't be safe."

"I live in Red Talons territory, and I'm standing up to them," Abel said. "Sometimes, you have to stand up, even when it's scary. In fact, when it's the most scary is when you most need to stand up. What happened to WW3D?"

"Don't WW3D me," Roa said. "Dr. Drago isn't afraid of doing scary things, but he's not stupid. And betraying my kin just to lose a battle would be very stupid."

"I don't plan on losing," Abel said.

"No one *plans* on losing," Roa replied.

"Look, if I don't win, my dad goes to jail for whatever crimes the winner wants to pin on him, and my mom becomes an *actual* criminal." Abel grimaced. "Plus, you know, I'll lose Karak, and the kin will be able to do whatever they want to him. Ally would easily hurt him on *purpose*, just to win."

"I know," Roa said, looking down at their knees. Their room was small, but it was filled with books about dragon care and dragon biology, and there were sketches all over the walls that they'd done of different devices for healing dragons. "I hated that."

"The Thunder Wings only study healing so they can get more work out of the dragons," Abel said. "They don't actually care what happens to the ones who serve them. None of the kins do. It's not right."

"Battling dragons *at all* isn't right," Roa said. "And yet we do it. So I think we're a little higher up in the air than simple right and wrong here. That's ground-level stuff. This is more complicated."

"Yeah," Abel agreed. Another thing about growing up too fast was seeing how much more complicated right and wrong could get . . . but some things, he knew, were absolute. Freedom was better than not-freedom. "Would it help if I told you I was gonna release all their dragons if I win?" he said.

"Release?" Roa sat up a little straighter.

"Set them free," he said. "Let them go wild."

"The Dragon Catchers will be after them," Roa said.

"We'll already be on the Glass Flats. They can get away from the city. Go wherever wild dragons go."

"We don't even know if there *are* wild dragons anymore."

"Well, there will be if I win," he said.

"Will the Wind Breakers kin let you do that?"

Abel laughed.

"What's so funny?" Roa didn't get it.

"There is no Wind Breakers kin," he said. "Not really. They're not, like, a gang with a leader. They're more a symbol for anyone who's fed up with the system. The other kin terrorize us and the Dragon's Eye controls us, and the dragons are forced to serve us. I'm doing something in the Wind Breakers name, but there's no one to give me permission or take it away."

"So you decide for yourself what the right thing is?" Roa said.

"Yeah." Abel nodded, watching his friend smile.

"That doesn't sound easy," Roa told him, "but it does sound good."

Abel matched Roa's smile with his own. "Awesome, because I'm gonna need your training on my ground crew, *and* your help outfitting Karak for the battle."

"Outfit with what?" Roa wondered. "You have some hidden arsenal of weapons systems under your bed?"

Abel took a deep breath. "What I've got," he said. "Is cab fare."

· · ·

Abel took Roa on his own back to the skyscraper where he'd stashed Karak, Grackle, and his dad. The kinner hostage was still tied up, but he had cake frosting all over his face and was taking a nap.

"Everything is better with cake," Abel's dad explained. "He hasn't caused any trouble since I gave him one."

Sippa took them to a long series of big rooms—some with walls, some where the walls had fallen away and were open to clear sky. But all, she promised, were filled with treasure.

"It looks like junk," Roa said.

"To a creative mind, junk is treasure waiting to be made," Sippa told them with a laugh that reminded Abel of the Wind Breakers' symbol. Before he could say anything else, she was gone up the stairs, and he and Roa were left in front of a huge floor of discarded metal and wires and . . . yeah . . . just junk. Maybe he didn't have a creative mind.

"You trained with the Thunder Wings," Abel said. "And they're the best inventors in the city. You had to have learned how to make some stuff, right?"

"I mean . . . yeah?" Roa said. "But the thing is, I can't do it alone. It takes a whole a lot of people and equipment to make dragon gear, *if* I can even find anything useful in all this."

"I'm ready to help." Abel's dad stood in the stairway door.

"And so are we." A group of people from the upper floor came in behind him. They were all different ages and from all different parts of the city, and they had tools with them, also of all different ages . . . some looked ancient.

"Me too," said one more voice coming down the stairs, hands his pockets, looking a little wary and a little embarrassed.

"Topher?" Roa gaped at him.

"I called him," Abel said. "I figured we needed someone with no loyalty to any kin. Someone who'd be glad to join the side of . . . chaos."

Roa was nearly speechless. "But he's such a—he's—a, uh . . ."

"Here to help," Topher said. "Unless you don't want it."

"No, we do," Abel quickly told him. "Thanks for coming."

He looked at Roa, trying to send his friend a message with just his eyes. *People are complicated*, he thought at them. *People can be more than one thing. And even jerks can do better.* Instead, he said out loud, "If Topher acts up, I can always have Karak cook him."

Topher laughed nervously, and Roa nodded firmly. "Good," they said. "Then he can stay. He better follow my instructions or it won't be the dragon he has to worry about."

"Are they always like this?" Topher asked Abel, but he was looking at Roa with a glint in his eye as he did. Roa didn't notice it, but Abel sure did.

"Just do what they say," he instructed Topher, and went to help his dad lift a heavy sheet of rusted metal off what looked like an old wrecking ball. Roa saw it and smiled.

"Someone get a piece of paper," they said. "I want to sketch out this idea."

Topher was there in a flash with his notebook and a pen. When Roa raised an eyebrow at him, he shrugged. "What? I keep a journal. I need to write down lyrics when I think of them or else I forget."

"You write lyrics?" Roa asked, and Abel saw a fleeting glint pass through his friend's eyes, before they stuffed it down. Roa looked away from Topher and grumbled. "I bet they're about racing dragons and farts."

"Well, the good ones are." Topher grinned.

Roa took Topher's notebook and got to sketching, their tongue sticking out the side of their mouth as they did. Abel's father had started directing some of the others to sort materials by type into piles. He even tried to do some of the heavy lifting himself, until Abel stopped him.

"Don't overdo it, Dad," he said. "Scaly Lung never really heals all the way."

"My son is about to fly a dragon against three well-trained riders who want nothing more than to destroy him," his dad said. "I can risk getting a little winded."

"Done!" Roa called Abel over eagerly, showing him the sketch they'd made in Topher's notebook.

"I suggested the nets," Topher said proudly, earning an eye roll from Roa.

Abel looked at the sketch. Roa had done a really good job drawing Karak and his saddle harness, and then added battle systems made from the scraps all around them.

"The systems are all defensive," Roa explained. "I don't want to hurt the other dragons, just make it so they can't stop you. His ankles have cuffs filled with metal shavings you can deploy to deflect incoming missiles; his wrists are gauntlets with magnets connected to a battery you control so you can turn them off and on to pick stuff up or knock it away. There's armor for his head and belly, and I turned all those old fan blades over there into a folding shield for the end of his tail. You'd control it with the same battery as the magnets."

"Just one battery to save on weight," Topher said.

"And because we only have one battery," Roa clarified.

Abel looked at the crisscross pattern all over the armor. "What's the netting for?" he asked.

"Close combat," Topher said.

"The armor is just the old tin there," Roa said. "And Topher made the point that it'd be too tempting for the others not to try to slice through it. Because—"

"Because it's where you look weakest," Topher said. "And bullies always attack where they think you're weakest." He paused and then added, "I know I did." Silence sagged between them until Topher took a deep breath and told them, "Sorry I've been such a jerk to you."

"We don't have time for sorries," Roa said. "Just prove you're not a jerk anymore."

Topher nodded and looked like he was genuinely relieved. He even smiled, and it was the first time Abel had seen a smile from him that didn't have any meanness to it.

"So the nets make the armor stronger?" he asked.

"All the old wires in that pile, woven together, are really tangly," Roa said. "Any claw that tries to swipe at you because they think your armor is weak will get their claws tangled up. And then—"

"And then Karak deals with them," Abel said.

"Yeah," Roa agreed.

Abel looked over the drawing again. They'd designed some pretty ingenious stuff from the junk in front of them. He looked at his two classmates, and at his dad, and at the odd assortment of Wind Breakers who'd come to help.

"No rider wins a battle alone, do they?" he asked.

"No one wins anything alone," Roa said. "Not really."

"What are we waiting for, kiddos!" Abel's dad clapped his hands. "Let's get building! We've got a dragon's outfit to make!"

"Dad," Abel groaned. "It's battle gear. Don't call it an outfit."

"What?" His dad grinned. "He's gonna look spiffy."

"And don't call my dragon spiffy!" Abel objected. "He's a ferocious battle beast who is going to save us all in righteous combat! He needs to look terrifying and indestructible!"

"He will, he will!" His father feigned innocence, then lowered his voice. "And also spiffy."

PART FOUR

"IT'S KIND OF A BAD LOOK TO
WHINE ABOUT FAIRNESS AT AN
ILLEGAL DRAGON BATTLE."

26

JUST BEFORE MIDNIGHT, STANDING BESIDE
Karak on the moonlit Glass Flats, Abel did not feel spiffy. He felt
sick to his stomach. Why did fear hit people in the stomach so
hard? Why not in the toe or the left ear? In answer, his stomach
clenched like it had just punched itself in the face.

Stomachs don't have faces, he thought, which made him laugh.

"You okay?" Roa asked.

"Not really," he answered, his laugh fading.

"Well, wings wide, losers, because it's on!" Topher slapped
him on the shoulder . . . hard. Abel gave him a look, but Topher
just grinned back. Topher was one of those boys who were so
out of touch with their feelings, even kindness came out like an
insult. He could only touch a friend by hitting him.

Abel turned around and wrapped Topher in a huge hug,
which froze the other boy in place. "Thanks," he said. "I really
love you too, bro."

When he broke off, Roa was laughing. Abel laughed too.

Messing with Topher really did make them both feel better.

"You two are such nerds." Topher sighed.

As they waited with Karak in his new junk-made armor, their
supplies for the battle set up in their spray-painted circle, they
all tried in their own ways to look brave. They also tried not to
look like they were trying.

Abel wished he had at least one adult on his side with him, but his mom had to stay home so that someone would be there if Silas or any other Dragon's Eye agents showed up asking questions. Abel's dad had to stay with the Wind Breakers in the crumbling skyscraper to guard Grackle, who they promised to release after the battle was *fairly* fought . . . or as fairly as a kin battle could be fought.

For the battle, Abel was dressed in jeans and a leather dragon rider's jacket that Sippa had given him. It was made from pieces of other leather jackets, stitched together with metal studs. The laughing dragon of the Wind Breakers was stitched on the back in metallic rainbow thread. The jacket had a high-banded collar to protect his neck, and the sleeves ended in metal guards that went over the back of his hands. Abel's thumbs went through holes in the leather so his palms were protected from what Roa called "rein burn." It was the coolest piece of clothing he'd ever worn, but it was kind of too big for him.

"I made your dad a promise," Sippa told him when she gave it to him. "That you would grow into it."

"Don't make a liar of her after she gave us cake," his father had added, his voice choked with tears. "Survive tonight. If it's a choice between losing the battle and staying safe, it's okay to lose. I'll be okay."

"No, you won't," Abel told him. "But I won't lose. And I *will* survive. I swear on a secret."

"On a secret?" His dad look confused.

Abel hugged him and whispered, "You're a great dad."

His father laughed. "Well, that's no secret! But I will hold you to this promise. Come back safely."

"I will," he said.

Now, standing beside Karak with his seventh-grade ground crew, he wasn't so sure he could keep his promise after all.

He'd been the first to arrive at the starting location, where the circles for the battle had already been spray-painted on the glass. They watched the others swirl in from the lights of the city skyline in the distance.

Sax rode a new dragon, a deep blue Frost Reaper with bloodred armor. Abel felt a chill race up his spine when the reaper landed and locked its ice-blue eyes on him. Sax took off his mirrored helmet and hopped down from the dragon, while his ground crew landed on their own wyverns and assembled their supplies. Jazinda herself had come to watch on the back of a short-winged dragon whose type Abel didn't even recognize, but was probably expensive. The kinners she'd brought rode dragons that were just as rare.

She frowned when Ally flew in on the back of the Ruby Widow Maker that the Thunder Wings had won from her kin. It took a lot of confidence to fly a brand-new dragon in a battle, and Abel wondered if his teacher was being *too* confident. Would the dragon see Sax and feel some old loyalty? Could Abel use that against her? Or was *that* a trick to try to get Abel to do something dumb? If he made a mistake, she'd surely use her new dragon to shred Abel to ribbons. He wondered what it would feel like to have jagged jewels tear him apart in the sky, fired by his former favorite teacher. Probably the same as if his least favorite teacher fired them, right? Once you were shredded by a dragon's breath, it didn't so much matter how you felt about the rider.

Ugh.

He was catastrophizing again, imagining the worst things possible and not being able to stop himself. He could almost *feel* the hot gems piercing his skin.

Topher, of all people, snapped him out of it.

"Relax," Topher told him. "If I managed to annoy her to distraction every day at school, you can do it for one night. Just ask yourself: *WWTD? What would Topher do?*"

That actually made Abel and Roa laugh.

"Watch and learn," Topher added, then called over to their teacher in the Thunder Wings' circle. "Instructor Ally! I'm worried the school doesn't pay you enough to afford the medical bills you'll have after Abel knocks you out of the sky tonight. You sure you should risk this on a teacher's salary?"

"Wow, that *is* obnoxious," Abel said, and Topher gave him a proud little nod.

"It's a gift," he said.

"Remember, kids," Ally called back to them, her voice like a claw scraping across glass. "I taught you everything *you* know, not everything *I* know."

"I don't think you scared her," Roa told Topher.

Jusif and Olus were Ally's ground crew. The Thunder Wings leader ignored Abel, but Jusif stared at him like he was trying to melt Abel's skin with his eyes. It might've worked too, but Karak snarled and Jusif yelped, then went back to readying supplies.

The last to arrive was the Sky Knights kin. The ground crew came in on their own little dragons, and Abel was surprised that their leader, Drey, hadn't shown up, even to watch.

He wondered if Drey would be their rider, but when he saw the first shimmer of their battle dragon flying out from the city, his heart sank.

It was the silver wyvern, that one that had been his brother's, the one that his sister had stolen.

And his sister was flying it.

She brought the wyvern in for a smooth landing on its two legs and settled it calmly in the Sky Knights' circle. The moment it stopped, she hopped down, tossing her helmet to her ground crew without looking. She strode toward Abel in her sleek Sky Knights jumpsuit.

"Hey, no secret sibling plots!" Sax yelled. He stormed over in Abel's direction too.

Ally, not wanting to be left out, made her way over. "I'm not sure Lina should be flying for the Sky Knights at all," she said.

"Yeah," Sax added. "What if they're in cahoots?"

"Who says 'cahoots'?" Roa grunted.

"Old people," Topher replied, and gave Roa a fist bump without looking.

"I'm not old," Sax snapped back. "I'm twenty-nine."

"That's old!" Jusif shouted from over in the Thunder Wings crew area.

"It kinda is," said Abel. "I worry about your back giving out during the battle."

"Good. You're learning," Topher told him, then said loudly: "I think Instructor Ally's in her midthirties. She might not even be able to stay awake for the whole battle."

"Enough trash talk," Ally snapped. "It's undignified. Of

course, I wouldn't expect dignity from a rat-eater like Topher. I'm surprised you'd keep his company, Roa. I thought you had better judgment than that. I guess I was wrong about you."

"Hey!" Roa objected, though they didn't add anything else. Abel knew this was hard for his friend. Roa had loved their teacher and didn't relish going against her. At the same time, Roa felt called to defend the wounded, and weird as it was, Topher counted.

"We're not in school here," Ally said. "Don't think I'll show mercy because I'm fond of my students. Though, for the record, I am." She looked Topher up and down. "Some of them anyway. If I can win without killing you, Abel, I will try to."

"Uh, thanks?" Abel replied.

"What about our objection?" Sax said. "Brother and sister can't fly for different kins. It ain't right."

"I have no problem going against my *little* brother," Lina said, making sure the word "little" landed with a sting. "He had the chance to join us, and he said no."

"That doesn't mean you can't be—" Ally said.

"In cahoots," Sax interrupted her.

Ally glared at him. "Working together against the other teams. I don't trust them."

"You were his teacher and you're going against him," Lina said. "How do we know you aren't in—"

"Cahoots," Sax interjected again.

"League," Lina continued. "In league. The Thunder Wings like clever little plots."

"And the Sky Knights will do anything for their cause," Ally said.

"And the Red Talons will destroy you all no matter what," Sax said. "We don't care who is in—"

"If you say 'cahoots' again, I'll knock the ugly off your face," Ally growled at Sax.

"League," Sax said. "Even if they are working together, we're still gonna win."

"No," Ally said. "We are."

"No," Lina said. "We are."

"No," Abel said. "I am."

"It's settled, then," Ally told them. "Lina can fly against her brother—*but* if it looks like you're going easy on him or letting him win, you forfeit."

"Fine," Lina agreed, and Abel wasn't sure how that made him feel. He didn't want her pity, but he also didn't want to battle her. "But if I can avoid it, I'm not gonna kill him either," she added. "He is still my brother."

"Well then," said Sax. "It looks like I'll be the only one trying to kill him." He smiled a toothy smile at Abel. "And maybe we'll make your dad confess to doing it himself once we win."

Abel shuddered. He looked to Lina for some kind of reassurance, mostly out of habit. She shook her head. "You boiled this water yourself. You gotta steam in it now."

"What is *that* supposed to mean?" he asked, but she was already walking away.

"Like a steamed bun," Topher said. "You know, like you steam buns over boiling water and they cook? She meant—"

"I know what she meant," Abel said. "I was just . . . never mind."

Ally sucked her teeth and looked at Abel sadly, then went back to her own dragon.

Sax was the last to leave. He towered over Abel, Roa, and Topher, then laughed a wheezy laugh. "Revenge will be sweeter than a sticky bun, and twice as gooey."

"Why do they keep comparing me to food?" Abel groaned. His stomach lurched again.

Topher shuddered. "Did that guy mean gooey as in, like, with our—"

"Entrails, yeah," said Roa. When Topher clearly didn't know what entrails were, Roa explained: "Blood and guts."

"Ah, great," said Topher. "Thought so. Awesome."

Not a moment too soon, Fitz arrived on his colorful dragon with its long white mane. He'd braided the mane tonight as well as his own beard, and he wore a very fancy black suit with gold and gray satin stripes. Abel smiled. He felt like that was Fitz's way of wishing him luck.

"Well, this is one for the ages!" Fitz said with high drama in his voice. "Brother against sister, teacher against student, Wind Breakers kin in its first battle, great riders facing off!" Then his voice dropped flat. "And also Sax is here."

"Hey!" Sax growled.

"Kidding, kidding, of course." Fitz let out a booming laugh that was so warm it disarmed Sax's anger. That, Abel figured, was how someone like Fitz managed to survive. He was impossible not to like. He also knew he couldn't fight other people's fights for them. He said so to Abel, in fact, at that very moment.

"Abel, I like you, kid, but I can't fight your fights for you. Or for your sister. I have to be impartial here." He waved at

Lina. "You know the rules and you know the stakes. Whoever gets the Wind Breakers hoard back to their circle first, wins. Got it?"

"Savvy," said Abel.

"Savvy," said Sax and Ally.

"Savvy," said Lina.

"Okay, Abel, as the challenger: Present your hoard," Fitz told him.

Abel reached into their supplies box and pulled out their hoard, one he'd made himself just a few hours ago.

Fitz smirked and held it up so the other dragons could see it clearly.

"Nope," Sax objected.

"Not a chance," Ally said.

"Really, Abel?" Lina asked.

"What? What's wrong with it?" Abel asked.

"It's a can of beans!" Lina threw her hands up in the air.

The only rules for what a battle hoard could be was that it needed the kin's symbol on it and it had to be precious. Abel had drawn the symbol on the can as best he could in permanent marker. As for being precious . . . he'd swiped it from the factory where he had first found Karak. It still had its label on it, Extra-Spicy Bean Paste. He figured that was fitting for a kin called Wind Breakers.

"It is precious to us," Abel explained. "To me and Karak."

"It has to be precious to *all* dragons," Ally said. "Otherwise, why would the others hunt for it?"

"Maybe because their riders are skilled?" Topher suggested, and Ally shot him a look that could've left bite marks.

"Sorry, Abel, but it's true," Fitz said. "This hoard won't work."

"But—"

"No hoard and he forfeits!" Sax was quick to say. "And the others fight it out for his prize."

"No," Abel objected. "That's not fair!"

At that, all the kinners laughed.

Fitz leaned over to whisper to Abel. "No offense, kiddo, but it's kind of a bad look to whine about fairness at an illegal dragon battle."

"But what do I do?" Abel whispered back. He felt tears pressing on his eyes, and an embarrassing lip quivering began. He pictured his father hauled off to Windlee Prison, his mother thrust into a life of crime, Karak sent into battle with a stranger on his back. He was doing it again . . . catastrophizing. He couldn't stop it. He'd messed everything up. He'd been reckless and foolish and impatient and—

"I have a solution," Jazinda Balk called out. A demonic grin showed her teeth as she stepped in between the dragon teams' circles. With a whistle, two of her goons brought a bound figure forward, stumbling.

His face was inside a child's drake-riding helmet, decorated with the logo of FiberBites Digestive Cookies for Sensitive Stomachs. Still, Abel recognized him instantly.

"Oh no . . ." Abel groaned.

"Oh brother . . ." Lina groaned.

It was Silas, in his green-and-silver uniform. Jazinda pulled out a sticker of the laughing Wind Breakers dragon and slapped it on his chest.

"This Dragon's Eye agent can be the hoard," she said, whipping off the helmet. Silas looked a little roughed up. He had a bruise on his cheek and his hair was all messy, which he'd hate, but he wasn't seriously hurt. He looked at Lina on *his* silver wyvern and tried to signal the dragon with his eyes, but Lina pulled the reins and she simply roared at her old rider. Silas winced. His pride would sting more than his bruises.

"There's nothing that says the hoard can't be a person," Jazinda explained. "And this one is precious to both Lina and Abel. As an agent of the Dragon's Eye, he's valuable to any of us. Plus, he would a make a tasty meal for any dragon."

"No," Silas said. "I'd be a terrible meal. All stringy and tough."

"Looks like a snack to me," Sax grunted, and his crew laughed.

"Not that tough either, I bet," Ally added.

"You *could* simply forfeit?" Jazinda suggested. "We can dispose of this young Dragon's Eye agent another way."

Abel looked around at the impassive faces of all the kinners, then to his brother and his sister. Finally, he glanced back to Fitz. "Fine," he said.

Fitz blew out his cheeks and shook his head, but agreed. "All right, then, on your marks!" He mounted his own dragon.

Jazinda's goons brought Silas over and hoisted him onto the back of Fitz's dragon like a sack of onions. Silas met Abel's eyes, and instead of looking angry or defiant, his big brother seemed utterly terrified. Abel was glad neither of his parents were here to see this.

"One more thing!" Abel remembered, yelling loud enough for the others to hear. "In order to win, the hoard has to be brought back to the circle *alive*. Otherwise he loses his value. The winner doesn't want to be stuck with a dead Dragon's Eye agent, right? Think of the bribes you'd have to pay!"

Fitz looked to the others for agreement. Lina nodded instantly; Ally agreed too. Sax, reluctantly, said, "Sure."

"Then here we go," Fitz said. "Look for the sign!"

He was off, flapping toward the city to hide Silas on a rooftop someplace all four dragons could hunt for him.

"Well, that upped the stakes, huh?" said Topher. "I mean, like, if you didn't need to win before, I guess you really do now."

"Shh," Roa hushed him.

"It's fine," Abel said, putting on his own helmet, testing the earbuds and scanning the skyline with grim determination. "I'm ready."

He wasn't, actually, but it didn't matter. He had to do it anyway. He was going to win this battle for his dragon, for his friends, and for his family.

Or he was gonna get knocked out of the sky trying.

ALL EYES SCANNED THE SKYLINE in heavy silence for what felt like forever.

"Hurry up . . ." Topher whined. "Waiting is the *wooooorst*."

"We can hear everything you say over the earbuds," Roa reminded him.

"Well, it *is* the worst," Topher said.

"Focus," Roa said, their voice comforting in Abel's ear. "You've got this."

"Do I, though?" Abel said back.

"WWAD," Roa replied. "What would *Abel* do? Win this *your* way."

"That sounds good," Abel said. "But what *is* my way?"

"You're the best person I know at—" Roa started.

But just then, the rainbow ball of flame burst into the sky, showering bright sparks above the tall buildings. Sax's Frost Reaper was immediately in the air. Ally's and Lina's dragons left their circles at almost the same time, breaking away in different directions. Abel was the last to launch, and almost as soon as Karak was off the ground, the Frost Reaper had looped back to attack.

A blast of frost so cold it froze anything it touched crashed directly into Karak's armor. If it had hit Abel, that would have been the end of his battle right then. But Topher's wire netting had a heating charge running through it from the battery. The ice that touched it melted almost instantly. Karak returned fire with a blast of flame that sent the Frost Reaper whirling away. Abel got them both clear, flying toward the city with some distance from the other teams.

"Karak is great!" Roa said. "With his starry camouflage and rusty armor, you can hardly see him at all. That's gonna be helpful."

"It looks like Ally is searching near our school," Topher said, peering through his binoculars. "And your sister is looking somewhere in the mid-city."

"Savvy," Abel confirmed. He steered Karak over the farm towers, trying to think where Fitz might have hidden Silas.

Smarts win battles, he thought. He had to remember everything he knew about his opponents and about Fitz. The Red Talons valued power above everything, so they'd try to let someone else find the hoard (it helped to not think of it as his brother), and then attack to steal it once it was found. The Sky Knights valued selflessness; they wouldn't hesitate to make Lina attack her own brother or brothers if they thought it would help them win for their cause. That meant she was probably trying to keep her distance from him. He believed she wanted to win, but she *probably* didn't want to come into direct battle with Abel to do it.

And the Thunder Wings valued knowledge most of all. Ally would search using what she knew about Fitz and about the other teams and gather whatever intelligence she could from as many sources as possible. She was a smart flier and wouldn't be easy to trick.

And then there was Fitz, who loved kids, and books, and laughter. Who knew about all the kins and was trusted by all. He was the kind of person who'd put on a fancy suit and braid his dragon's mane for a battle. What did that tell Abel?

Abel smiled. He had an idea where Fitz had hidden Silas. It was the braids. Fitz had told him back in his store.

"Mad Hazel the Marauder braided her dragon's mane when her enemies closed in," Abel said into the mic. "She also burned down her own house."

"What are you talking about?" Roa asked.

"Clues," Abel said. "I think I know where the hoard is, but I don't want to fly right there or the others will see. I need to distract them."

"Only one way to distract a dragon in a dragon battle," Roa said.

"A battle!" Topher added eagerly.

"Yeah," said Abel. "I got it, thanks."

He leaned forward. Abel felt the warmth of Karak's scales against his chest and cheek, and he watched the city racing by below. "Here we go," he told the dragon, and then leaned and pulled the reins, steering Karak straight in Lina's direction.

"You're going after your sister!" Topher yelled into Abel's ear. "That's hard-core!"

Abel didn't answer, just kept racing toward Lina on her wyvern. His sister looked up, startled. Her ground crew must have told her he was coming, which was what he'd hoped would happen. He dropped Karak lower between the buildings, catching his streaking black reflection in the glass on either side of him. He pulled back on the reins a little so that Karak opened his mouth, showing the blossoming orange fire like he was ready to attack.

Lina moved to avoid him, racing down another street, and Abel rose up over the nearest skyscraper and dropped down in front of her. She had to make a sudden turn in the other direction to avoid him, heading straight for Ally on her bright red Widow Maker.

Abel was sure his sister could take care of herself, and the moment the Sky Knights and the Thunder Wings started battling, he knew the Red Talons would be along, thinking one of them had found Silas . . . er . . . the hoard.

I can't think about him as my brother, he reminded himself. *Or I'll never have the nerve to snatch him up in my dragon's talons.*

He hoped Silas wasn't too afraid right now. Though after the way he'd acted to Lina, Abel, and their parents, Abel wouldn't mind if his big brother peed his pants a *little* before the battle was over. Glancing over his shoulder as he raced through the streets, he saw that no one was going near the spot he thought Silas had been hidden, and that made him smile. His trick was working.

And then WHOOOSH!

A blade sliced right past his head, so close it scratched the plastic of his helmet. Karak swerved, and the next blade whistled straight through the air where his chest had just been. It buried itself into the steel of the building next to him.

"Where is that coming from?" Abel yelled.

"Hey, don't yell into the microphone!" Topher yelled.

"Red Talons dragon perched on the side of a building at eight o'clock," Roa said.

"What? What does that mean?"

"Like on a clock?" Roa said.

"I can only read a digital clock!" Abel replied.

"*Everyone* can read a digital clock!" Topher said. "Duh."

WHOOSH! WHOOSH!

Two more blades whizzed past him, and he had to weave and dodge. Three more were incoming, but Karak used the gauntlets on his wrists to knock the blades away in a shower of sparks. A blast of frost erupted from a spot in the middle of a bright red ad for Passionfruit Wyvern Wafers. The dragon was using the hologram as camouflage! Abel steered Karak to dodge the frost, but the breath weapon had just been a distraction. The Frost Reaper dove from the glowing light of the billboard, its wings wide and its talons up, slamming into them.

The impact alone almost knocked Abel off his saddle. It rattled his head in his helmet and his skull in his head.

Karak screeched, and the Frost Reaper roared, and Abel did his best to hold on as the two dragons went jaw to jaw and claw to claw in midair. Just like Topher had planned, Sax's dragon got its talons caught up in the netting around the tin armor. Abel hit the button that increased the electric charge.

"RAAAAAAWR!" the frost dragon screamed. Abel could practically hear Roa wincing through their mic. They'd planned the shock to be no harder than the NERDs got in school, but they'd had to raise the voltage for trained battle dragons.

"Shut it off!" Roa shouted.

"Yeah, don't use up the battery," Topher said. "You might need it later."

Abel shut it off, but the other dragon had been weakened

enough that Karak got a good slash across its armor, opening an exposed patch of blue-and-white belly scales—the weakest part.

"See you at your funeral, kid!" Sax shouted from the back of his dragon. He pulled out a small lightweight crossbow and aimed it right at Abel's chest.

BOOM!

He never got the shot off. A sonic grenade detonated right next to Sax with such force he fell sideways off his saddle, clutching his head. At the same moment, Karak shot a blast of flame into the open part of the frost dragon's armor. The Frost Reaper thrashed so hard it snapped free of Karak's netting, then dove away between two buildings in a wild-eyed race toward its pit crew back on the flats.

"Close one," Abel panted, breathless. But he didn't have time to recover, because it was his sister who'd launched the sonic grenade, and now she was diving straight for *him*. For someone who said she didn't want him dead, she sure was flying at him like someone who meant to take his head off.

The wyvern's mouth opened, a cloud of poison gas growing in its cheeks.

"Just give up!" Lina shouted.

"What about our parents?" he shouted back.

"This is bigger than our family!" she shouted. "This is for the liberation of all *Drakopolis*!"

"You care about your cause more than your own family?!"

"I care about it more than my own life!" Lina replied.

"That's not what I asked!"

"Just give up!" she yelled again, then pulled back the reins to slow her wyvern. She fired a small burst of poison, just large enough to stun Abel.

Karak bent his tail as Abel pressed the button for the fan shield. It snapped open and blocked the spray. The move forced him lower, however, toward late-night short-wing traffic. Taxis and buses dove out of the way, their passengers screaming in their seats.

Lina dropped down, racing beside Abel. She weaved in and out of the traffic, shouting over at him.

"Give up!" she repeated. Her dragon rammed into the side of Abel's, trying to make them crash. He glared at her and tightened the reins, speeding up. She bumped him again. He bumped her back as they weaved through traffic at dizzying speed.

"Abel, Ally's coming straight toward you!" Roa warned in his ear.

He looked ahead and saw his old teacher on a collision course. Her big red Widow Maker flew full speed to intercept him! The dragon's mirrored helmet gleamed, and its mouth opened to fire its jagged breath weapon.

"What do I do?!" Abel yelled.

"Stay calm!" Roa yelled back. "Remember your OODA loop."

Abel *observed* the buildings to one side of him, his sister to the other, the pavement below, and the open sky above. He *oriented* himself, speeding straight toward the armed dragon his merciless seventh-grade teacher was flying; then he *decided* what to do.

It was time to *act*.

"Here we go, Karak," he told his dragon. "Let's do this." He ran a hand along the warm scales of his neck, making the spiral pattern. He felt the dragon hesitate, and he squeezed tighter with his thighs. "Don't worry," he said. "I got us this time."

The dragon snorted and snapped his wings shut, then dove, turning his neck at the same time to curl his body around itself. The speed of the motion turned into a spiral, and Abel felt the skin pulling back on his face, the g-forces increasing as they whirled in a tornado of wing and scales. The buildings blurred around him and then—the moment before they hit the hard concrete of the ground—Karak opened his wings. They shot forward from the spin with such speed that Abel's whole body left the saddle. His hands lost their grip . . . but his harness held.

He'd remembered to clip the safety strap.

He used the strap to reel himself down onto Karak's back, straining every muscle in his arms against the g-forces. They were flying faster than Abel had ever imagined. They left the other dragons in their windy wake. Karak let out a loud whistle as he flew. The dragon was *enjoying* himself.

In spite of it all, so was Abel.

He whooped as loud as he could.

They bolted like lightning just above the ground, as the two dragons behind them tangled into one another.

"You're injured!" Roa told him.

Abel touched his neck. He was bleeding a little. He must have been grazed by a gem from the Widow Maker or broken glass from a building. There were a lot of ways to get hurt in a battle.

"I'm okay," he said, wishing his friend hadn't told him. Now he noticed the sting and began to wonder how much blood he'd lost.

"Karak's armor is torn open, and the netting is ripped," Topher said. "If they catch up with you, you're pretty defenseless."

"Come back for repairs," Roa said.

"I can't," Abel replied. "I'll just get in a fight again and lose. I need to end this."

"They're after you," Roa said. "Ally and your sister. They're also fighting each other, which is slowing them down, but you don't have a lot of time."

"Good thing I don't need a lot," he said, which he thought sounded cool.

He headed straight for his own apartment building. There, on the roof, was his brother.

"Thanks, Fitz," Abel said under his breath, so quiet not even the mic would pick it up.

Silas had his hands cuffed behind his back and his legs bound together. He was propped up against the ledge of the building. At least Fitz had been kind enough to put the helmet back on him.

Abel had Karak swoop down and scoop Silas up in his front claws as gently as a dragon could.

"I got you, big brother!" Abel shouted as he dove between the buildings, racing back for his circle on the Glass Flats.

"AHHHH!" Silas screamed, which Abel figured was as close to a thank-you as he would get.

"Your sister and Ally are still behind you," Roa said. "But they're waaaay behind."

"What about the Frost Reaper?" Abel asked.

"It left the repair pit," Topher said.

"And? Where is it?" Abel's heart sped up, which he didn't

think was possible. It was already racing as fast as a human heart should.

"I don't . . . I . . . um . . ." Topher mumbled. "I lost it."

Abel burst over the roofs of the tall farm buildings. In the distance, he saw the three circles where the teams stood on the glass. He and Karak left the city lights and dove across the dark glass, skimming just above the surface, tracing its waves and whorls, the smooth dunes and jagged cracks.

He was a heartbeat from victory.

Which was exactly when the huge blue Frost Dragon in bright red armor dropped down in his path, its mouth open to ice him.

"FIRE!" ABEL SHOUTED, PULLING THE reins. Karak reared back, wings wide and gleaming with starlight. The dragon loosed a hot blast of fire that hit the incoming ice in midair.

As the ice and fire slammed into each other, they created such a sudden cloud of vapor that the air cracked with thunder. Mist enveloped Abel and Karak, along with Sax and his dragon. The force of the Frost Dragon's breath pushed against Karak, but Sunrise Reaper's fire pushed back just as hard. The dragons were locked together, exhaling ferociously. Abel wasn't sure who could do it for longer.

He thought about his DrakoTek cards. Frost-spitting dragons had a +2 against fire breathers . . . and if the cards were right, then Karak was going to run out of breath first!

Knowing that, Abel knew he had to control how the battle ended, instead of letting Karak exhaust himself.

In the cloud, the Frost Dragon was just a shadow, but the huge temperature changes in the air would trick any heat-seeking goggles Sax had on. Abel and Karak were nearly invisible to him—and to the ground crews below.

The Sky Knights only understood power. They wouldn't stop attacking until Abel was destroyed, so Sax probably couldn't imagine a defensive retreat so close to victory. Abel could use that against him. He snapped the reins, and Karak broke off his fire breath. At the same time, Abel steered Karak to lean all the way backward, belly to the sky, rotating in a full backflip.

"Hang on tight!" he shouted to Silas. A blast of ice shot through the mist, just over Karak's belly and over Abel's brother, who was gripped there.

"AAHHH!" Silas screamed.

They rolled through the loop-the-loop. Abel held on for his life, grateful for the safety harness. They came out of the flip just below the mist cloud, with Silas a nose's length above the hard glass ground.

They streaked forward with three massive wingbeats. Karak dove to their circle, sliding Silas onto the surface as gently as Abel's mom slid a pancake onto a plate. Then Abel turned in a quick circle and came in for landing himself.

Sax was still up in the cloud he'd made, searching for his opponent. Ally and Lina were only just arriving over the Glass Flats, both of their dragons looking the worse for battling, neither having defeated the other.

Fitz sat on the back of his dragon. He pulled at the reins, and the dragon launched its rainbow fire, signaling the end of the battle with a shower of rainbow sparks.

"Wind Breakers win!" he yelled.

Roa and Topher charged forward, cheering.

"That was incredible!" Roa helped him down from Karak and hugged him.

"Unbelievable!" Topher joined the hug, surprising even himself.

"Nice flying, bro!" Lina yelled from her own circle. Drey and the other Sky Knights were busy yelling at each other for not even seeing when Abel had grabbed Silas off the rooftop in the first place.

"Losing kin!" Fitz announced. "Surrender your battle dragons to the winner and abide by the terms of your bet. All debts owed by Abel and his family are forgiven."

Jazinda looked like she had just smelled a fresh pile of dragon dung, but she nodded. Sax led his Frost Dragon to Abel and presented the reins. Ally did the same, and so did Lina.

"I'll expect Grackle returned to the Half-Wing by morning," Jazinda said.

"My dad will have already released him," Abel replied. "If he's walking now, he should make it across the city by sunrise."

Jazinda grunted. "You've got guts, Abel," she said. "We'll honor the terms of the bet. But I've got my eye on you. Remember that."

The huge dragons towered over Abel. Karak eyed them all warily, then looked down at his rider, waiting. The other three dragons looked down at him too. Abel held four long leashes in his hands. He had four powerful dragons that suddenly belonged to him. They were a little scraped up from the fighting, and panting from the exhaustion of the battle, just like he was.

"You won them all," Topher said. "This is amazing. I think we have more dragons than any seventh graders in history."

"No," Abel said. "We don't have any dragons."

"What—what are you—" Topher pointed up at the dragons. "They're, like, right there, Abel! Do you not see them? Did you crack your helmet? Is it a concussion? DON'T FALL ASLEEP!"

"I mean," Abel explained, "Karak won the battle, not me.

And it wasn't even his fight. It was *ours*. People's. It's not right, battling them this way, keeping them this way, making them fight for us."

"But—they're dragons!" Topher said, his voice cracking. "Fighting's what they do."

Abel shook his head. He looked at Roa, who gave him a small nod of agreement. He hoped Topher would understand. He was just starting to like the guy and would hate to see him go back to being a bully. But even if he didn't understand, this was what had to happen. "I'm letting them go," he said.

One by one, he unclipped the armor and the leashes from the dragons he'd won. Abel bowed to each of them, like he'd bowed to Karak when they first met.

"You're free," he said. "All three of you. Go to the wild. Live as you were born to live." The dragons blinked down at him. "Go!"

"Abel," Ally told him. "Dragons aren't *meant* to be free. You really should have paid more attention in class."

"I won, and I can do what I please with these dragons," Abel snapped back at his teacher in a way he never before would've dared. "And I am setting them free."

"But . . . but . . . we won!" Topher whined.

"You better do it fast," Roa said. "The law's coming."

They pointed, and Abel saw a long line of Dragon's Eye wyverns racing from the city toward the Flats.

"It's the Eye!" Jazinda shouted. "Scatter!"

"Savvy!" her Red Talons replied. Suddenly, there was a rush of movement as all the kinners scrambled back to their dragons and melted away into the night.

"See you around, kid," Sax snarled. He climbed on the back of another Red Talons' dragon as a passenger, and the two flew off.

"Better get a move on, Abel," Fitz said. "You don't want to get caught out here."

He too flew away into the dark.

"I am not going to jail again because of some snot-nosed, comic-reading kids," Ally grumbled. Olus and the Thunder Wings loaded up their dragons to flee. "But I will see you all back in school," she added as she left.

It sounded like a threat.

"I think our grades are gonna suffer because of this," Abel apologized to Roa.

Roa shrugged. "There are more important things than grades."

"You're way cooler than I thought you were," Topher told them. "But if you let these dragons go, we're gonna be powerless."

"Their power isn't ours," Abel said. "We just borrowed it for a while. I want to give it back." Topher didn't try to stop him. Abel shouted up to the dragons looming over them, "Hey, dragons, go! Go on!"

He tried waving his arms at them, but they just stared at him. Then, as one, they looked at Karak.

Of course. Karak had won, which made him the alpha dragon, just like in class with the ERDs. They'd do whatever he did, which meant Abel had to convince his own dragon to leave first.

He had to say goodbye.

"Karak, thank you." Abel undid the saddle and heaved it off Karak's back. "It's been an honor to fly with you, but you need to be free."

Karak lowered his face to meet Abel's, just like when they'd first met. Abel set his palms flat against the warm snout. "You can't stay. They'll lock you up in a stable again and make you battle. You need to go now. Your wings are your own, and they should take you wherever *you* want, not where people tell you to go." Karak bumped him a little and grunted. "No, not even me," Abel said.

The dragon snorted; then he reared back up to his full height, opened his wings, and screeched. Roa and Topher flinched, but Abel stood tall in front of Karak. He raised his hand to wave goodbye. Karak bent his legs and thrust himself into the air with a roar. The other dragons watched him rise, and then, with their own terrible roars, followed him, circling overhead.

"Wings wide, my friends," Abel whispered after them. "Wings wide."

"Abel," Lina sighed. She looked back at her own kin, who were waving frantically at her to go. The Dragon's Eye were closing in. "You made a lot of powerful enemies tonight."

Abel looked up at the dragons as they finished their circle and flapped away into the darkness. Dragons flying free and wild—how long had it been since that last happened? He smiled and wiped a tear away. "Yeah, but I made some powerful friends too."

Lina shook her head. She backed toward her kin, hopping on a running dragon as they all disappeared back toward the lights and crowds of the city.

"So, uh, how are we gonna get out of here?" Topher asked. They were three kids, alone and dragon-less on the Glass Flats, with the Dragon's Eye just minutes away.

"They don't have any proof we were involved in the dragon battle," Abel said. "Except for Silas."

They all turned to look at his brother, who was still on the ground. He'd lost his helmet in the landing but was sitting up with his hands bound behind his back. His hair was a mess, and he had a nasty scrape on his forehead. He had an even nastier expression on his face.

"You want me to cover for you *again*?" Silas snarled. "Why should I?"

Abel thought of a lot of insults he could hurl at his big brother right then, but there wasn't time. The law would be on them soon. If he and his friends were going to stay out of Windlee Prison, he had to make peace with Silas, and he had to do it fast.

"Because you're not nearly as dumb as your face makes you look," he said.

Ah well. He couldn't resist. Roa elbowed him, and he tried again, nicer.

29

"I *DID* SAVE YOUR LIFE," Abel reminded Silas.

Silas grunted.

"And if they do arrest me, I might *accidentally* tell them how you covered for me last time, making up that story about Lina taking me hostage," Abel added. "You'd get in trouble too."

"You wouldn't," Silas said, but there was doubt in his voice.

"Come on." Abel tried a more pleading tone. "You've been as helpful as hot sauce in a hard drive since all this trouble started, but you could actually do something good now."

"You want me to break the law," Silas snapped. "Then I'd be a criminal, just like you and Lina. No thank you."

"You'd be a *hero* to Mom and Dad," Abel added. *That* got his brother's attention. Silas sat up a little straighter. "They'd be so grateful to you for protecting me, for doing what they couldn't. I bet they'd get you those new riding gloves you wanted for Saint George's Day. And I'd owe you too."

"You *already* owe me," he said.

"I'd owe you more," Abel replied.

Silas thought about it.

"We don't have all night," Topher warned as the Dragon's Eye wyverns grew larger on the horizon. They'd spread out in a wide V to block any chance of escape.

"Fine," Silas said. "Untie me and I'll cover for you . . .

again. But you have to do whatever I say, and not contradict *or insult* me."

"Well, I can't promise that I'll—"

Roa and Topher gave Abel looks as hot as Karak's breath. He shut his mouth and nodded.

Roa went to Silas and undid the knots at his wrists and ankles. Abel's brother pushed himself up from the ground and neatened his hair, trying to look dignified. It was only moments before the swarm of Dragon's Eye agents swept in around them, landing in a circle, with more dragons flying overhead.

"Hands above your heads, palms up! This is a law enforcement action!" a voice blared over a speaker. "NOW!"

Abel raised his hands in the air, as did Roa and Topher.

The Dragon's Eye agents circled them. In the dark, the glowing green eyes of their night vision goggles made it look like they were surrounded by fireflies, until a spotlight lit them up from somewhere high above and he saw their uniforms and their weapons and the ferocious sneers of their dragons.

From the back of a bright green wyvern, smaller than the one Lina had stolen, Kai rushed over to whisper with Silas, pulling off his night vision goggles as he did. He nodded toward Abel and then pointed off into the distance. Abel wondered how he'd explain the Sunrise Reaper that had wreaked havoc throughout the city, without revealing that Abel had been the one flying it. But Silas was, Abel had to admit, no dummy. From the looks of it, Kai believed whatever story his brother was telling.

As they talked, another agent approached and handed Silas a fresh Dragon's Eye coat. Silas slid it on smoothly, straightening the stiff collar and rubbing the rank insignia. Abel wondered how long his brother had been a Dragon's Eye agent while the rest of his family thought he was an Academy cadet. Just like with Lina, there was a lot more going on in Silas's life than Abel had known about.

Unfortunately, Abel was about to know more.

Silas reached into a pocket and took out a phone. He tapped the screen and made a call, turning his back away so Abel couldn't even see his lips move. As Silas talked on the phone, Kai came over to Abel.

"Hey, Kai," Abel said. He started to lower his arms to wave, when another agent shouted.

"KEEP YOUR HANDS UP!"

Abel obeyed, though his arms were exhausted from the battle. It seemed ridiculous to make them stand like this; they were three seventh graders who were unarmed and totally surrounded. But you didn't argue with two dozen Dragon's Eye agents whose wyverns had enough poison breath pointing your way to knock out every person you'd ever met in your life.

"So . . . Lina was here?" Kai asked him.

Abel didn't want to give too much away, because he didn't know what story Silas was telling. He just grunted without committing to an answer. Kai pursed his lips and looked kind of disappointed. Then he turned and waited for Silas to come over.

"It's handled," Silas said.

It had only been about a minute since the Dragon's Eye arrived. Abel couldn't believe his big brother worked that fast. He looked at his friends, who still had their hands up and were just as confused as he was.

"Um . . . okay? What now?" Abel asked him.

"You three were witnesses to some serious crimes," Silas explained. "You're also children. The Dragon's Eye has no interest in sending you to Windlee Prison, but you will serve your community nonetheless."

"We will?" Abel didn't know where his brother was going with this.

"You work for me now," Silas said. He took a deep breath and ran his hand through his hair.

Topher let out a whimper.

"Oh, it's not so bad as all that," Silas said. "It's okay, you may lower your hands. Just move slowly." Abel hated how much of a relief it was to be given permission by his brother. One of the wyverns narrowed its eyes at him. There was a glimmer of glowing green behind its rows of pearly white teeth. He couldn't keep his hands from shaking.

"After tonight, you and your friends have the attention of every dragon battler in the city," Silas said. "The Dragon's Eye can protect you and keep you out of prison, of course, in exchange for your services."

"Our services?" Abel asked.

"Congratulations." Silas grinned. "You are now officially informants for the Dragon's Eye. You'll infiltrate kin activity and report back to me about everyone involved and everything that happens."

"You want us to be snitches," Topher said, sounding miserable.

"Think it of it as undercover operatives, if that makes it sound better. But yes, you'll be my snitches." He brushed dirt that wasn't there off the shining Dragon's Eye pin on his collar. "That call I was on was to the school district. Needless to say, your old instructor will *not* be returning to her teaching job. It seems she's a fugitive again. You might want to keep an eye out for her, though. I imagine she'll hold a grudge."

Abel couldn't even think of an insult for his big brother. He was almost grateful, but also outraged, and terribly confused too. He had become, in short, quite nonplussed.

Topher, however, found the words to say exactly what Abel was thinking. "What? Um. Like? Um? What?"

"Do a good job as my operatives," Silas said, "and we'll all just forget about what happened here tonight. Do a bad job, and . . . well, there's always room in Windlee Prison."

"And Lina?" Abel asked. "What about her?"

"She's a wanted criminal," Silas said, "and she *will* be caught. It's Drakopolis. No one escapes justice forever." He gave Abel a cadet's salute, his fingers bent into a claw against his chest. "Welcome to the good guys. Your code names are TBD."

"What's TBD?" Topher asked. "Which letter am I?"

"It means 'to be determined,'" Roa explained.

"Right, I knew that," Topher muttered toward his shoes.

"Ugh, please don't make our code names stupid," Abel groaned.

Silas just grinned at him, then walked to the circle of wyverns. He and Kai and climbed aboard the green one.

"Ep ep," Silas barked. The dragon bent its legs and leapt straight into the air, the rest of the Dragon's Eye wyverns leaping up after it. The spotlight shut off and left them blinking in the dark.

"Wait!" Abel shouted at the sky. "How are *we* supposed to get back to the city?"

"Better start walking!" Silas shouted down. "It gets hot out here once the sun comes up!"

Moments later, Roa, Topher, and Abel were alone on the Glass Flats, so far from the city they couldn't even hear its rumbles and roars.

"So . . . did we just get . . . recruited by the Dragon's Eye?" Topher marveled.

"Guess so," said Roa.

"I hope I get a cool code name," Topher said.

"Knowing Silas, you won't," Abel sighed.

Topher shrugged. "I do kinda like their uniforms. And they have the best battle dragons, right?"

"I just set four dragons free. I don't want to *battle* new ones. I want to *free* new ones."

"Well, maybe we still can," Roa said brightly, clearly trying to cheer him up. "Maybe this is how we do it. Infiltrate the kin, like Silas said, but also the Dragon's Eye. Play them against each other, and we can bring them all down from the inside."

"Bring them down from the inside?" Abel snorted. "I'm sure that's what everyone who ever got eaten by a dragon thought they could do too, just before they got swallowed."

"Dark," Topher grunted. "Now I'm hungry."

"I have a Wyvern Wafer," Roa offered.

"Share!" Abel begged.

The three of them started walking back to the city, sharing a candy bar under a gleaming moon and more stars than anyone could count.

When he looked back over his shoulder, away from the city lights, Abel thought he saw a few of the stars slide across the sky in the shape of dragon's wings. He smiled.

It might not change the world or solve his family's problems, but there were four dragons flying free who hadn't been free before.

As small as he felt between the huge night sky and the huge city ahead, that thought made Abel feel a little bigger.